THE NORMAL MAN

THE
NORMAL
MAN

Susie Boyt

WEIDENFELD & NICOLSON
London

First published in Great Britain in 1995 by
Weidenfeld & Nicolson

The Orion Publishing Group Ltd
Orion House, 5 Upper Saint Martin's Lane
London WC2H 9EA

A catalogue record for this book is available from
the British Library

ISBN 0 297 81531 8

Typeset at The Spartan Press Ltd
Lymington, Hants

Printed and bound in Great Britain by
Butler & Tanner Ltd, Frome and London

Grateful acknowledgement is made for quotations from the following:
'Maybe It's Because I'm a Londoner' (Hubert Greg) © 1947, Reproduced
by permission of Francis Day and Hunter Ltd, London WC2H 0EA
'Are We To Part Like This' (Harry Castling/Charles Collins) © 1912,
Reproduced by permission of B Feldman and Co Ltd, London WC2H 0EA
'Oh I Must Go Home Tonight' (Will Hargreaves) © 1936, Reproduced by
permission of B Feldman and Co Ltd, London WC2H 0EA
'If You Were the Only Girl In the World' lyric reproduction by kind
permission of Redwood Music Ltd, UK administrator in respect of the
Estate of Clifford Grey
'What She Is Writing' by Stevie Smith from *The Collected Poems of Stevie Smith*
(Penguin Twentieth-Century Classics) and James MacGibbon
Anna Karenina by Leo Tolstoy, translated by Rosemary Edmonds (Penguin
Classics, 1954) copyright © Rosemary Edmonds, 1954. Reproduced by
permission of Penguin Books Ltd.

With thanks to

Ian Bostridge
Isabel Brunner
Daisy Cockburn
and Joey Cunningham for
Nobody's Children

.

For Robert

Chapter 1

My grandmother was a beautiful cook. She could bake a cake that you'd swim the channel for. Only she scorned icing. It seemed frivolous to her, and because of this her cakes never received the recognition they deserved. Children did not give her baking a second glance. People who inclined towards high-street fashion or fancy dress passed them by. They were always the last to sell at the summer fête or the Christmas bazaar. Yet those latecomers who did buy them or the occasional polite guest who ate out of a sense of 'waste not, want not' found her cakes so delicious, if they were discerning, that they would fall silent and close their eyes while they ate in order to feel entirely awake to the taste. But it was more than taste. They were so soft and airy. 'Mountain breezes blew within them,' my father said. If there was fruit it was bursting at the seams with the plumpness that came from a night's soaking in some favourite tincture. If they were sponge and sandwiched with a little raspberry jam their yellow height seemed to defy gravity and the rich smell of vanilla scented the room.

To my grandmother, icing was lacking in moral energy. It was too worldly. It was an excuse for a cake's poor inner life, denoting some anxiety on the part of the baker or an insufficiency on the part of the consumer who demanded it. Only the true intellectual or the pure in heart amongst her acquaintance saw that the worth of her cakes lay beneath the so-sad appearance of their nude surfaces.

I tell you this because it seems to catch something of an important dynamic at work in my family.

The competition in the women's magazine was in three parts. You had to write a profile of your heroine, a short essay on Sex and the Single Girl and a 'think piece' about the family. Janey March liked to enter competitions. It was something that she and her father had done together when she was a child.

The kind of competitions Janey usually went in for were of the slogan variety. 'My ideal man to take on a Star Cruise to the Greek islands would be . . .' in no more than twenty apt and original words. Janey had some idea about her ideal man, he probably had a sweet tooth and liked going on buses and mending things, he might play football on Sunday afternoons, and have a liking for cups of tea which she would make for him but it was all a bit uncertain. If the competition read 'The last person on earth I would like to take on a Star Cruise' she would have been spoilt for choice.

Last month she had written a jingle for a chain of in-store baked potato outlets called Spuddies which she was particularly pleased with: 'At Spuddies . . . we cater for every taste in potata.' The prize for that one was a three-minute trolley dash at Price Cuts. But the talent contest was giving her more trouble. The prize was three months' work experience on *Together* magazine and the closing date for entries was in two days' time. Sex and the Single Girl was proving to be rather a stumbling block. The articles *Together* usually ran advised you how to please your man: Perfect your gravy – Make time for sex – Don't let depression get you down

– Send off for maribou-trimmed lingerie – Keep off wheat and dairy products to achieve a smoother line – He's working late? Surprise him at the office with an all-over body massage. That sort of thing. Very contrived and unromantic. But worst of all, this way of thinking went against the ideas set out in *Good Love? Bad Love?* by Rocky Lorrio which was Janey March's bible. She took it everywhere with her and knew its first paragraph off by heart.

> *Good Love is when love is the icing on the cake of your life. Bad Love is when love is the cake, the plate, the table and the floorboards. Good Love is about Choice. Bad Love is about Need. Good Love is sharing, giving and taking. Bad Love is giving or taking. Bad Love is always passing judgement on yourself and others. Good Love is about owning your own and others' worth. Good Love, despite the myths, does not make you ache, shake, sick, nauseous and afraid. Good Love feels like coming home.*

Janey had made a note to herself, in pencil, in the margin. 'NB. That people can be dismissive about icing is hard to believe when the frequency with which it is employed in figures of speech suggests that as a substance it must have more meaning than is generally allowed.'

It was six o'clock on a Friday. Janey lit the gas and put the kettle on. She found days off difficult, although she had decided that she must spend the first ten days of the summer holidays away from any sort of work.

Usually she would think of interesting things to do, rare films and pictures to go and see. She would make expeditions to tucked-away shops that sold exotic items at low prices: twisted foreign breads with bitter seeds and herbs baked into them; paper lanterns and multi-coloured birds made from feathers; garish rose-printed fabrics; scented bubble bath with mysterious powers that could also be used for washing steps; sorrel, sporrans, sepia greetings cards; shimmering 3D pictures of the Virgin Mary. She would have a cup of tea in Soho with a college friend; visit a market stall that sold only gingham whilst humming 'Maybe it's because I'm a Londoner'. She would stroll round the National Gallery and linger over the pastries in the chilled cabinet in the café, thinking 'What's the fastest cake in the world? Scone,' and laughing to herself. But she often felt, on these days, while the rest of London was at work, like an insensitive parent dragging a reluctant, moody child around the city.

The day before she had taken herself off to a viewing of Olivia de Havilland's clothes which were on show at one of the South Kensington auction houses, but again she had found the experience disappointing. The rows and rows of two-pieces and gowns, set out simply on plastic hangers dangling from a picture rail, all *couture*, all Dior, all the same size (Olivia de Havilland obviously hadn't been up and down with her weight) seemed overwhelmingly drab. The greys and the greens and the strange old-fashioned shades of blue were so reminiscent of the charity shop and the jumble sale that if it hadn't been for the certificates authenticating their celebrated owner and their various outings (the party after *This Is Your Life*, the Canadian premiere of *Gone with the Wind*, the Academy Award ceremony) and of course the silken white and gold labels that announced their pedigree, they might have belonged to anyone's old grandma. The grey Going Away suit worn after her marriage, for instance, with wide pleated skirt and tailored jacket, looked like what a bus conductress might put on in the morning, but only for everyday wear, not if she was on nights or if she had her eye on one of the drivers at the depot. The wedding dress itself was glamorous, but this was because it was made from silk satin the colour of champagne roses. It was very very plain. If you couldn't allow yourself even a tiny flounce or furbelow on your wedding day then when could you? There was a red A-line woollen dress and a peach evening column with gold belt and cap sleeves which were almost chic, but most of the garments left Janey cold. There was no glamour to them at all. No doubt they were intended to be modestly beautiful, individual poems to understatement, but they had failed in this by being dreary, and when you thought that they must have cost an arm and a leg each — it seemed dishonest, uninspired and wasteful.

On these outings, supposedly undertaken for pleasure, Janey often longed for her work. Her thesis on Jane Austen was to be continued after its triumphant first sentence. '*The response that Jane Austen's novels invite is at odds with what their author actually reveals them to be.*' But there were still three months to go before she was even meant to begin it at the start of the next term and she didn't want it going stale.

It had been a very long day. She had been woken by the ringing of the telephone in the early morning.

'We need to talk,' said her actor friend.

'Go on then,' she said.

'I need to see you person to person.' They agreed to meet at nine thirty on the steps of the National Gallery. Janey glanced at herself in the bathroom mirror and did not like what she saw. The actor liked women to be calm and serene. A fat shiny spot with a yellow head perched on the edge of her cheek. 'Bloody ugly cow,' she said out loud.

She rinsed her face, making a bowl with her hands, filling it with water and flinging it against her cheeks. She drew off her nightdress and put on her best pair of white flower-patterned knickers and a pair of dark blue trousers. She fastened the hooks of her best bra under her breasts with the cups at the back and swivelled the apparatus round until it was in place, feeding her arms through the straps. She put on a navy T-shirt that she had worn the day before. Then she sprinkled talcum powder on to her hair to absorb some of the grease and sprayed some scent into her armpits. She looked in the mirror again and the face in the mirror curled its lip.

Perhaps there was time to wash her hair. She hung

her head over the side of the bath, put the warm tap on and worked up a lather with Country Girl shampoo, whipping the long brown strands into soft peaks and mounds of white froth before she rinsed them and wrapped them in a towel. With her hair piled on top of her head like that her father used to say she looked like a Sultana. She took off her shirt and trousers and put on a floppy white skirt that was now two sizes too big for her, securing it with a safety pin. She slipped into the crisp white shirt she kept in her wardrobe for emergencies, interviews, funerals, not that she ever attended any of these events. She liked wearing white clothes.

So there she was, standing on the steps of the National Gallery, breathing in the dry heat of Trafalgar Square, presiding over the pigeons, watching the passers-by and the back of Nelson's hat, wondering what it was he had to say.

The first time she had met the actor it had been in a café with a mutual friend and he had been in a very heightened state because he had just escaped from a lift in a nearby department store which had got stuck between the fourth and fifth floors. For twenty-five minutes he had stood in the dusty Otis lift – designed for not more than ten persons or 1600 pounds – with an old lady, a younger woman and her small child. (He took frequent deep breaths as he related the adventure, and you could see the darkened smoke-filled café was like a hillside pasture after the airless interior which had trapped him.) It had impressed Janey, his retelling of the scene; his slight stutter and the trembling of his

hand as it held its coffee cup or cigarette lent his words a
certain shyness. He had been touched by the child's
generosity in handing out all her sweets in the crisis and
the old woman's tale of getting stuck up an oak tree as a
girl, during the war, chasing after her wayward
tortoiseshell cat; and then the younger woman had
joked about the whole episode being masterminded by
her husband in order to prevent her from 'not another
shopping spree, Miriam'. Then, they'd decided, he
said, the four captives in the Otis lift, they had joked
and planned that if they ever got out alive they would
hold a reunion in the same lift in a year's time. And the
voices he had done – still somehow retaining his air of
diffidence although he had been talking uninter-
ruptedly for nearly ten minutes now – sweetness and
light for the little girl, slightly stern and knowing for the
old lady, bustling and lively for the young mother; it
was all so charming and festive, such an attractive
mixture of confidence and unconfidence that she had
wanted to kiss him there and then.

So they had started seeing each other in a casual sort
of way. He had something of a cavalier attitude towards
time and places and people, which she did not share,
but they made each other laugh and she cooked him
bakewell tarts and brought him endless cups of tea, and
at night they drank Irish whiskey together. But it was
never very easy, not for her at any rate. The day after
they had spent an evening together he would telephone
and set up a postmortem on her behaviour, outlining
how she'd gone wrong, fiercely critical, letting her

know how she could have arranged things better and how, exactly, he would have liked her to have acted in the circumstances. Once they went to visit an aunt of his, who had made them a cake, and Janey had declined a piece even though she had been pressed several times to accept just a small bit, and this had made him furious. Their conversations often began with an unspoken accusation from him hanging in the air.

'Please don't be cross,' she said. 'I just wasn't hungry. And anyway, eating cake isn't a happy thing for me, it's something I do to cheer myself up. I wouldn't do it out of choice.'

'I do love you, Janey, and I always will,' he said, 'but I can't help thinking a lot of things you do are really terrible.' He grew more angry and silent whenever she became upset by his words. 'Oh, you mustn't mind me,' he'd say, cross that she didn't defend herself more effectively against him. He was forever telling her what she should not mind and this was what she minded most. The writer of *Good Love? Bad Love?*, she vaguely knew, might have suggested that her liking for him fed on some lack in herself. But he was such a good actor. On stage he achieved a level of articulacy and intense emotion that surpassed anything he could muster at other times. In fact she had occasionally seen something heroic in the fact that as far as she knew he did not choose to act offstage more often, when it would obviously have made his life more manageable.

Twenty-five minutes past. Her hair was almost dry.

She pulled a comb through it and the tangled strands stretched and snapped between the fine teeth until they shone. He was always half an hour late and she was always five minutes early; it was a bad joke between them that neither of them would change. She could see him now, walking across the square, and she put the comb in her bag. She always saw him before he saw her. She waved at him and he met her on the step and kissed her hello.

'Why do girls look prettier when the sun shines?' he said, stroking the side of her head. She shrugged her shoulders and they went into the gallery together. Inside it was the same as it always was with him in such places. She looked at him and he looked at the paintings. They followed each other round but she did not want to be seen to do so and now and then she would hang back or dart into another room when he was not looking in case he should feel claustrophobic or that she wasn't her own person. But it was in him that her interest really lay. How could a painting hold more allure than a real person, flesh and blood? A room that was filled with some of the most famous Impressionist pictures in the world could seem unremarkable, somehow cloying, unreal. But the way the light fell on him in the room, and colours of the clothes he was wearing; the grainy texture of the skin on his face and the shadowy folds in the fabric of his long-sleeved T-shirt where he had rolled up the arms, even the yellow ochre tobacco stains on his fingers, seemed intricate and touching. The paintings were all very well, but to look at them with care and to look at him, the whole thing would have been too rich.

They left the gallery after an hour and threaded their way up Charing Cross Road until they got to a café they knew off Tottenham Court Road. Janey sat down while the actor bought her a cup of tea with money she lent him. He looked her in the eye with a quizzical slant to his expression.

'I think we should be friends.' Whatever they had been to each other they had never been friends.

'Friends instead of what we are already, or as well as?' she asked.

'Instead of.'

'OK, then.'

He kissed her on the lips. 'I'll be in touch,' and before he had quite finished the words he had slipped away into the sea of sale-crazy sofabed shoppers and hifi seekers and rib eaters and the small crowd that had gathered outside the School of Scientology and Dianetics. The good people of Tottenham Court Road. Janey finished her tea. She felt terrible. She rolled up the arms of her shirt. It was going to be a blisteringly hot day. She strolled down Tottenham Court Road until she got to the Dominion. And there standing on the corner was a young man in a heavy overcoat. He was positioned near the curb but although the illuminated little green figure was beckoning him across the road, he did not stir. There was no expression on his face although one hand cupped his forehead and his mouth hung open. His other hand was caked with

12

blood and dirt. He lowered his eyes to the pavement and shook his head slowly from side to side. He was standing in a small puddle of urine. Janey looked at him stood there under the heavy cloud of some impossible pain in the city heat. She had never seen a man look so lost to himself and his surroundings. She went up to where he was standing. She formed the words in her mind that she would use towards him: Can I get you anything? She took a pound coin out of her purse. Have you got somewhere to stay? She knew the whereabouts of three hostels within walking distance, she had helped out at one of them the Christmas before. She could buy him a cup of tea and a cake somewhere, maybe she could get him to go to a day centre, maybe see a resettlement worker or something. He was looking at her now.

'You all right, love?' he said, cheerfully.

'Fine,' she said, startled, and nodded her head to swallow up embarrassment.

'You sure?' She nodded again.

'And you?'

He nodded too and fished a pair of sunglasses out of his pocket and put them on. He took a few shuffling steps back to the theatre and leant back against one of the thick glass doors. Janey paused for a few moments and then she walked away.

She knew that it was a well-known fact, probably a named psychological phenomenon, that people were often disappointed by the predictability, the triteness of their own responses. You could see people by the dozen clicking their tongues and rolling their eyes when they found themselves humming 'Singin' in the Rain' the moment it came pouring down. Janey herself sometimes dreamed that she had lost her baby and was running through the streets shouting 'My Baby, My Baby!' and looking in houses and under cars and yet she could not find it, and she had run down alleys and dodged through a council estate and out into the country over hills and green pastures, through fields of cows and sheep and foreign corn, into an old barn, shouting 'My Baby, My Baby!' and into some farm buildings (My Baby!) and up some stairs into a child's room (My Baby!) where she tore back the bedcovers to reveal . . . herself, Janey March, large as life and twice as ugly. You didn't have to be Sigmund Freud to work that out. And yet here she was outside the Dominion telling herself that it was worth bearing in mind that whatever trifles might afflict her she was not a man like that wearing a great woollen coat on the longest day of the year, and never would be.

There was a supermarket round the back of Covent Garden and she made her way there, walking quickly, jogging and then sprinting down Shaftesbury Avenue and up Neal Street, across the piazza, past the Canadian Muffin Co. and the bank and into the new shop. And there it was, arranged in little bustling avenues, tiled with black and white, rich with piped hot crusty-bread smell and freshly squeezed orange flavour; bitter with citrus floor cleaner, cloudy with frosted fridge air and then hygienic smell-lessness in between. All expertly lit and crammed with shining eye-level produce in arresting packaging. There was scope for endless combinations and situations: each green fruit might be the apple of your eye, even a ready dinner might win you some undiscerning person's heart. All that plenty. Janey loosed a trolley from the stack and let it take her down each aisle as she admired the view on either side, stopping when a new line caught her eye, up and down, round and round, putting her weight on the vehicle and letting it take the strain. There was a pay phone conveniently situated by the entrance to the shop so that you could phone your loved one and check which two veg he wanted with his meat. Looking at it she felt a great pang of longing for the actor whom she had often phoned from supermarkets.

'Where are you ringing from?' he'd say.

'Frozen peas,' she'd reply. It made her feel alluring somehow to ring people from unexpected places. 'To be a *femme fatale*, develop a laugh that is both alluring and dismissive,' she had read in a magazine. Sometimes she practised this in the bath. Ha; uh ha ha; uh ha uh haha. She mustn't ring him, though. Poor thing. Give him a break. Into her trolley she put butter and eggs and sugar and cocoa and flour and icing sugar and the evening paper.

Two boys from Courtleigh Boys school had won a certain amount of fame a few years back, Janey remembered, by arriving at a supermarket bearing clipboards, wearing grey suits and wheeling a trolley to

15

which a red ribbon had been attached. Approaching a likely-looking old woman, they had said, 'Congratulations, you are our millionth customer, you have won a three-minute trolley dash.' Then, guiding the beribboned handlebar of the trolley into the old girl's hands, they had shouted, 'Your time starts now!' and the old woman had gone berserk, cramming it with everything in sight, and the two boys had just sloped off leaving her to face the music at the checkout.

There was one person in the queue at the 'eight items or less' and while she waited Janey surveyed the small pile of items on the ledge to the left of the till. Generally Janey liked to choose something from this sorry selection of near misses but the choice today was particularly uninspiring. Three tins of peas, a chocolate swiss roll, a box of eggs with runny yolk seeping through the cardboard and several bags of fruit which had not been weighed and would require further queueing at the other end of the store. Janey paid in cash and with her bag of goods, her cake in the making, she walked briskly back to Charing Cross Road, caught a 29 at the lights and as it halted and jerked its way along the streets to Victoria she hatched her plan. Back home in the kitchen she would lay the ingredients on the table, grease three bun trays, find forty-eight crenellated-paper cake cases, drop a large teaspoon of cake mixture into each case, place the cases in the tins and that would make forty-eight little cakes. She would take them to the man at the Dominion. But would he still be there when the crowds assembled for the Moscow Circus or whichever lavish musical was playing? It would say in the paper. She drew the paper out of the carrier bag and came face to face with a small picture of a handsome man with saucy grin and big appealing eyes. Black letters were balanced on his head. CAN YOU GIVE THIS MAN A BED THIS WINTER? Winter seemed years away. Underneath were the details of a local charity for single homeless men. The bus drew into Victoria. From the top deck Janey watched the to-ing and fro-ing of people in the weary travellers' no man's land. It was not a place of rest. Everywhere there were passengers, for the coach station, for the bus station, the trains, the Gatwick Express to the aeroplanes, the boat trains and the taxi ranks and the parcel delivery depot. Even the people who had nowhere to go seemed to swing between the triangle of rail station, McDonald's and the bricked forecourt of Westminster Cathedral.

Janey got off the bus as it moved into the bus station and walked along Victoria Street, disappearing behind the Cathedral into the terrace of mansion blocks in which she lived. Home. She phoned the number of the centre that was asking for help.

'Hello,' she said, 'I wonder if you can help me. I had to make a lot of cakes today and I made too many. Could I bring them round later or doesn't it really work like that?'

'Sure,' said the woman at the other end. 'Cakes would be great, thanks.'

Janey set to work. Twelve ounces of best Normandy unsalted butter – these men weren't going to have to eat cakes made with margarine on top of everything else, if she had anything to do with it – twelve ounces of sugar: cream together until the mixture is pale and fluffy. It was murder on the wrist when you did it properly. Then three eggs, twelve ounces of self-raising, eight ounces of cocoa and then milk to get it to the right consistency. Each batch fourteen minutes in the oven, test with a skewer, cool on a wire rack, smooth over shiny chocolate fudge icing (sorry, Granny, but I never knew you) layer into two cake tins with four over which she would keep for emergencies. Snatching food from the mouths of the homeless. But what if the homeless didn't want her baking? She ran her finger round the edge of the bowl and put it in her mouth. The icing tasted rich and sweet.

The best combination of personality a woman could have, a magazine had told her, was tough and sweet, not so good for food though.

She raced down the four flights of oatmeal-carpeted stairs, with the two brightly coloured cake tins stacked in her arms, like a child's drum. She walked to the St Bartholomew's Drop In where she handed over the goods; then she took back the tins and walked home again.

In her absence the postman had been. One of the good things about entering competitions was it meant you received a huge amount of junk mail which forced the postman to call. Her address must have been sold time and time again. For some reason bulky envelopes addressed to the 'Good Food lover of Musgrave Mansions' often landed on her doormat. It was a plain doormat. She had once been given an 'If It's Bills, We're Out' doormat by one of the women who had worked in the theatre with her father, but it had been packed away somewhere.

Dear Miss March,

WHO WANTS TO BE A MILLIONAIRE?
£3,000,000 GIVEAWAY

Is the *March* household heading for success? Are the fortunes of the *Marches* about to take a turn for the better? In years to come will people look back on the *March* dynasty with the same green eyes that they view the Gettys and the Rockefellers and say 'Ah, it all began when *March, (J),* won the lottery? Do you, *Miss March, (J),* want to be a millionaire?

This was the sort of thing she had laughed at with the actor. He had read similar entry forms to her in a grating quiz-show-host drawl. He was very good at accents. She remembered him announcing a Match the Meals to the Country competition. Chow mein, Haggis, Burger and Fries, Pizza and Sauerkraut were listed and he had read the name of each dish in the accent of the country that it was least likely to have come from and had her in stitches.

Sometimes when they were finding it difficult to get

on in an ordinary fashion she and the actor would slip into American accents and talk for hours on end about the concerns of an American couple they had invented, Beth and Mork, whose relationship was subject to constant domestic upheaval.

In their fantasy, Mork worked nights at a taxi rank and Beth would phone him there and quiz him (casually) about the ladies of the night who patrolled the precinct by the cab office. He would grow edgy and evasive at her enquiries, and, for revenge (Beth thought), he would deliberately forget to pick up the groceries she requested from All Nite Al's. To get him back, Beth had embarked on a series of half-hearted infidelities with the men who came to fix things in the house, for things were always going wrong in Beth and Mork's house. Getting wind of this from the guys at the diner, Mork would respond by, say, deliberately ignoring Beth's latest hairstyle, not complimenting her on her new outfit, failing to notice the lace-trimmed 'intimate apparel' she had bought with him in mind. Then Beth, slamming and fuming, would throw off her apron and grab the phone to dial for divorce. While the line was ringing (It's ringing! It's ringing!), Mork would come to Beth and look at her with those big eyes of his, and she would melt and in the blur of her swoon he would gently tease the phone from her fingers, saying, 'Honey, we just gotta stop tearing each other apart.' Then Beth would bite her lip, tuck her hair behind her ear and whisper, 'You take care o' me,' and Mork would say, 'I take care o' you,' and they'd kiss and make up.

But when they couldn't quite get on in an American accent, sometimes they could feel quite friendly towards each other in a sexy Maurice Chevalier sort of broken English, where they said 'Zank Evan for zat' a lot. And when that didn't work they would speak in a West Country burr, which accompanied the fantasy they shared about one day opening a bed and breakfast by the seaside called The Fag and Apple.

'I baint be 'avin no wife of mine calling bingo numbers of an evening,' he'd say when they discussed new ways of cashing in on their guests.

'Don't you go telling me the wheres and whyfores,' she'd reply.

And when they just couldn't get on at all they would speak in French. She'd heard that there was a certain French philosopher who believed that the most perfect analogy that existed in the whole world was that between ten times four and forty, and when they spoke in French, this was the sort of thing that they discussed. In all the other voices they used they were married or as good as, for some reason, but in French they spoke as virtual strangers. She knew French quite well and he hardly knew it at all and this somehow made their communication easier, made the fact that he didn't understand her seem less troublesome, just a language barrier. Right now she felt a pang of longing for him that transcended any geographical consideration. It was very tempting to ring, but she must hold out a bit longer.

*

The kettle boiled and Janey made a cup of Earl Grey, burning herself slightly as she scooped the last teabag out of the hot water with thumb and finger. She sat down at the kitchen table with her cup. On the edge of the piece of paper on which her piece about her grandmother was written she made a list:

1. Have a cuppa. (She ticked this off.)
2. Decide what to wear to Lucy's party tonight.
3. Get forty winks.
4. Forget Him. (Next to this she wrote Forget Who???!!!)

She was tired now and feeling restless. She decided to wear whatever to the party and try to leave reasonably early. She had the address on a scrap of paper: Flat 1, 28 Wordsworth Gardens. She hated Wordsworth, he was the actor's favourite poet. Twenty-eight: a little duck and a fat lady. She did not much feel like going out this evening. She tried to get herself in the mood by having another cup of tea. It didn't work. She read her stars in *Together* magazine:

> *Someone you meet on a routine bus journey at the weekend will change your ideas about love.*

She lay down on her bed for an hour or two and at eight fifteen she woke, changed into a blue stretch velvet T-shirt and matching mini skirt and applied a glamorous make-up to her face. Concealer, foundation, powder, mascara, lipstick and rouge on the apple of her cheek. She had tried to achieve a sort of Snow White look. 'You'll do,' she said to the face in the mirror. She saw the yellow head of her spot winking at her through a heavy layer of Hide The Blemish: 'Just.'

Going to a party was about the last thing on earth she felt like doing. What she really felt like was working, she found it relaxing and stimulating, it held her interest and made her feel happy, whereas going out was stressful, tiring and often a disappointment. But she had to go. You had to put yourself about a bit in life and, anyway, not to go would be rude.

Janey March had been well brought up. She had not stumbled up like some of her friends, learning the different ways there were for going about things from the television or the teachers at school. She had been actively taught by her father's example to keep others in mind, to help those who were less able than she was, to make them feel at home when they were ill at ease, to be helpful, tactful, generous, to see the best in people, to define herself through acts of kindness and, when she did wrong as all members of the species did, to shoulder her share of the blame. Her father's good nature, his delicacy, grace and understanding were much more than policy. He would not for instance have located these traits in himself, they simply stemmed from a desire deep in the heart of him to do what was right, to render good for evil, when it was within his power. He liked the idea that all his actions had a nodding acquaintance with the sort of principles embraced by Levin in *Anna Karenina* (one of his heroes), not in any extravagant way, just in the normal run of things.

Generosity of spirit was just a part of him, as his right arm was, or his eyebrows. It was second nature to him to avoid all mean practices which when he saw them made him sick at heart. But as well as being something of a delicate man he was also surprisingly resilient. Although his skin had a thinnish appearance like that of a young girl, and his features were fine, his smile was big and easy, his eyes were of a deep blue and inclined towards humour, his hands were large and smooth. He could look after himself all right, but he was wholly unassuming, easy-going even, take it or leave it, play it by ear.

'What's for pudding, Dad?' Janey asked the man in the blue and white stripey apron and matching stripey oven gloves, as he pulled a roasting tray from the oven which held a hissing side of beef framed by a garland of golden roast potatoes.

'It's wait and see pudding tonight, sweetpea.'

In the tunnel that led to the Victoria line at Victoria Station an old man was singing. His voice was loud and echoey as he crooned away, swaying from side to side, swinging his arms about.

'Maybe it's because I'm a Londoner
That I think of 'er wherever I go
I get a funny feeling inside o' me . . .'

His striped shirt, blue trousers and the scarf that was knotted round his suntanned head made him look like a fancy-dress pirate. Janey dropped a fifty-pence piece onto a jacket which lay at his feet. He stopped singing and gave her a funny look. He changed his tune.

> *If you were the only girl in the world*
> *And I was the only boy*

He was singing straight at her. Janey lingered at his side. People were staring, but:

> *Nothing else would matter in the world today*
> *We would go on loving in the same old way.*
> *A garden of eden just built for two la la la*
> *La la la laaaa.*

He stopped singing. 'I think I'm falling in love with you, Pal.'

Janey took a step back, 'Oh dear, I don't think my husband would like that.'

'Big fella, is he?'

She nodded, 'Very big.' She raised her eyes to the roof of the tunnel to indicate this.

'Ah well, no harm in trying.'

'No harm at all,' she said.

'God bless, Pal. Keep safe.'

'And you.'

'Going somewhere nice?'

'I'm going to a party.'

'Don't do anything I wouldn't do.'

'All right, I won't. G'night.'

His voice rang out loud and echoey down the tunnel.

> 'I would say such wonderful things to you.
> There would be such wonderful things to do

If you were the only girl in the world
And I was the only . . .'

She boarded a waiting train, counted up the stops to Highbury and Islington on her fingers and opened up *Good Love? Bad Love?*.

> *As plaque is to a tooth, so Bad Love is to the heart, destroying, weakening and decaying the body's natural defences.*

Chapter 2

Janey often felt lonely at parties. She had admitted before now that she didn't like going to big parties on her own because you ended up talking to the radiator. She leaned against the broad arm of the pale sofa at Lucy Harrison's house-warming and felt just how much she was longing to have someone to be different with. Someone to walk down the market with (Tachbrook Street, Berwick Street, Portobello, even Inverness Street would do) and buy vegetables to make soup. Someone to serve blackberry and apple crumble to, once autumn came.

If she had some new love interest she could make steak and kidney pie for him and they could walk up to Hyde Park while it was in the oven and go on the boats. She thought back to a party she had attended a week or two ago. She had feared things might be winding down with the actor; and done up to the nines in a new dress that lent her a considerable cleavage, dressed to kill (and on the pill), newly free of a large amount of excess weight and a little giddy thanks to three months of very strict dieting, there had been at least five men whom she could have taken a shine to and yet none had seemed to show any interest at all. Her friend Kate had said, 'You looked so frail, maybe they thought you'd have a nervous breakdown if they forgot to ring you or something.' It was true, though, if people thought you had 'Handle with care' stamped on your forehead they wouldn't touch you with a barge pole.

Janey's 'Sex and the Single Girl' competition entry was going round and round in her head.

> *A woman's desire to become involved with a man can have some sort of commerce with feeling unhappy. It is a symptom of a larger malaise. If you lack the strength to carry on self-sufficiently, minding your own business, fulfilled and serene in the knowledge that you are a going concern all on your own, you can look abroad.*

But you could get nice steak and kidney in the butcher's in Pimlico for £1.77 a pound, it was on special offer, she happened to know, and she imagined a man eating it in her kitchen off an oval plate on a red and white gingham tablecloth with sun streaming in through the windows and a bunch of white flowers that he had brought her standing in a milk bottle.

The tall man who had sparked off this reverie was standing to her right on the other side of the deep cream sofa, apparently unaffected by the machinery of her thoughts. A red warning light was flashing WRONG WRONG WRONG in Janey's brain but she hoped she might be able to summon all her powers of concentration to dim its glare or transform the now-neon sign worthy of a top name in show business into something more positive. You could change one letter at a time. Wrong, prong, print, paint, saint, pains, rains, ruins . . . but she could not get it to be RIGHT. It was no good.

But the tall man had definitely seen her. She had caught him glancing at her for a second or two. The third time he casually cast his eyes her way she saw him wonder if she had noticed him. He looked tired and not really in the party mood. They were standing in a large cream room with two uncurtained windows framing a tidy row of terraced houses opposite. Double doors, one opened, one closed, gave onto a smaller candlelit kitchen area. There was little furniture in the larger room, only two pale sofas and two tables, each item placed against a different wall making four little comfort stations for rest and refreshment.

There were a few men in suits who were largely shadowed, creased and tired around the eyes. Other men had shorter hair and the influence of sportswear in their clothes. There were some women in short skirts which wrapped their thighs like bandages, others wore a longer length split skirt which the magazines were calling 'the new silhouette' and some wore jeans and stretchy tops. The two tables supported between them a tray of mini pizzas, some colourful sliced vegetables, carrot, broccoli, cauliflower, radish, mangetout, midget corn and little boiled potatoes, with pink and white dips and a couple of emptyish ashtrays as well as glasses and bottles. A woman with red hair wearing green and a woman with blonde hair wearing a short A-line baby pink mohair dress stood out, the latter sort of swaying from side to side as she looked out onto the street scene. Janey watched her drunkenly stumble and descend into the deep cushioned sofa that was positioned between her and the man. There was something annoying about the way she was sitting; she was trying too hard to be fetching, putting too much energy into being curvaceous or something. Frank Sinatra crooned across the room. 'You'd never know it, but buddy I'm a kinda poet and I've got a lot of things to say.'

The woman in green came and sat next to the blonde girl, took her hand and squeezed it. 'D'you know the joke about the boring party?' she asked. The girl in pink shook her head. The girl in green said, 'Two ladies at a cocktail party, one says to the other, "Boring party, isn't it?" The other says, "I know, I'm going to go as soon as I can find my knickers."' The girl in pink laughed feebly.

'How's the Mark situation?' the girl in green asked.

'Terrible. He range me fourteen times last night. I mean, why doesn't he give me a hard time?'

'Don't you like him at all then?'

'I do like him. But not like that, and he doesn't seem to be getting the message. And then he says the most pathetic things like, "You'd be upset too if you had a broken heart."'

30

'Maybe you shouldn't have gone home with him that night.'

'I know, but it was so funny though. We were at the pub and it was last orders and he said, "Will you come home with me tonight?" And I said, "What?" And he said, "Will you come home with me?" And I said, "Don't be funny." And then he goes, "Please come home with me, just this once, no strings."'

'And so I say, "You can't just expect people to go home with you because it's Saturday night and you've had a few drinks." And he says, "I know, don't be like that, I just thought it would be nice, that's all. Oh please." And I said, "NO. N–O spells NO." And he said, "Pleeeease?" And I said, "Oh go on them, I'll get my coat."'

Both girls fell about laughing. Janey smiled. Sex and the Single Girl. She wondered if the tall man was smiling too. The girl in pink's hair was so blonde, it was like a tiny child's. Janey had been born with hair that colour. From an early age her mother had instructed her on the benefits to be gained from the application of camomile shampoos and rinses to her hair (they had, after all, kept her mother's hair yellow). She had used these preparations regularly to safeguard her daughter's crowning glory, washing into the child a mild alarm at the prospect of any change. But less than a year after Mr March had died, when Janey was twelve, her hair was as brown as a nut.

Janey's concentration drifted back to the tall man. He seemed to be listening in to the conversation of the two girls, as she had been. He was so good-looking, it was almost ridiculous, the kind of man that if you had been sitting down and you suddenly saw him, it might have made you fall off your chair. As he listened she thought she saw him look at her briefly and she in turn traced the shape of his upper body whilst peering at him from the very corner of her eye: his dark brown hair and his large light eyes of some colour that she could not see, his slightly too big, but very characterful nose, his wide mouth in a happy grin, his chin, his shoulders, his chest in its blue or black shirt full of cotton with floppy collar and light brown buttons, three little sandy islands. She wondered how tall he was, probably six three. She wanted him to look at her now. She crossed the sofa, passing the talking girls and him to get to the table that held the drink because she felt like a drink to calm herself down, and the journey was an advanced obstacle course of stockinged legs and sofa legs and men and table legs and her own two legs all threatening to become intertwined unless she took the most careful of steps. She poured herself a glass of sparkling wine, peering at the bubbles that hissed and fizzed at her. 'I know just how you feel being bottled up all that time,' she told them. She wanted more glamour in her life, that was it. The two girls were still talking.

'You know Emma's new boyfriend?'

'Yeah?'

'Well she says she met him at a party, but I think she met him through the Lonely Hearts.'

She was almost certain that the tall man wasn't

looking at her now. She stood sideways on to the table with her back to the man. She placed her left leg straight out in front with the foot turned to the left and the right leg about six inches behind it with the foot turned out to the right. It was the most flattering attitude you could stand at legs-wise. A magazine had told her; but the same columnist had advocated smudging lipstick onto the earlobes to reflect a healthy glow on to the paler complexion and once a friend had caught her doing this and shouted with astonishment, 'What the hell are you doing?' She wondered if the tall man was ignoring her on purpose.

Perhaps he has a cruel streak, she thought. Janey knew, she had read, she had been told that the kind of man she was drawn to often turned out to be a little cruel to her. Nothing major at first; gentle put-downs, sternish criticisms of the way she went about things, not that she didn't exactly deserve it, but they could have used more kindness in their voices or wrapped her up a bit more in their arms afterwards, she always thought. That men liked her best when she made an effort to be happy, clever, pretty and funny she could understand, but what surprised her was that they liked her best when she criticised them . . . and although there was nothing wrong with that in itself . . . actually, it did seem wrong to her if people wanted you to be unkind. For her part she wanted more than anything to be able to give a man what he himself lacked, not to take away the little he did have. To give him confidence to help him believe in himself. So she would be encouraging and supportive to men and they would behave appallingly, interpreting every attention as an oversight, believing that it took less effort and imagination to be kind than it did to create the intimacy and excitement that accompanied a fierce analysis of their shortcomings. She wanted them to see the goodness in themselves that they were blind to, bolster them up a bit, remove the mistrust in them that was the source of their severity, but again and again it seemed like this was the last thing that these men with the sharp corners and the hard edges wanted.

Before the actor there had been a Scottish man with a piercingly earnest face and frank red hair who sneered at her for liking avocado pears and called her Lady Di because she lived in the centre of town. He laughed at the clothes she wore, telling her she looked a mess, or like an unmade bed or an accident in her red and white flowery summer dress. He called her Drearie as a term of mock endearment, when she did not make more of an effort with her appearance, but when she got herself up for a party or an evening out and put on a bit of make-up, just a little lipstick or something to bring out her eyes, he said she looked like lamb dressed as mutton.

But he was so clever. His favourite way of spending the evening was for them both to lie in a candlelit room where he would tell her about art and history and the wonders of mathematics and science and literature because he knew all about these things, and she would listen silently, refilling his glass and emptying his ashtray until he fell asleep. Then she would cover him with a Black Watch blanket, slip a pillow under his head, smooth his red hair with the flat of her hand for a few minutes and then kiss him on the temple goodnight. He could charm the birds off the trees when he wanted to, but in his most tender and drunken moments or when he was wearing tartan, he would say, 'You'll never be my ideal woman because you're not my mother,' and shed a tear for 'the three of them'.

She'd cooked meals for him when he was sitting his finals, bringing round a tray of food to his room on the Camden Road with a starched linen napkin and a yellow rose, all the way from Victoria on the 29 bus. 'That for me? Oh, you shouldn't have, babe,' the conductors would say. She'd typed out his thesis at short notice, staying up all night, because he kept changing his argument; he hadn't even chosen to celebrate with her when by this joint effort they just managed to reach the deadline, preferring instead the company of his ex. Three months earlier, when she herself had been busy with her own work on Emily Brontë's poems, she had helped sew a whole cast of costumes for *The Tempest* when the actor had turned his hand to direction, and he had never thanked her, never even referred in passing to the work she had done. It wasn't that she wanted him to be overwhelmed with gratitude but she would have liked to have been able to tell him how the blue and silver feathers on Ariel's costume had floated up her nose and made her sneeze as she stuck them on and how her head had reeled and she had nearly passed out from the fumes of the glue. In time both these men had invited her, had begged her to confide her weaknesses to them, saying, 'We'll never get anywhere unless you do.' And she, taking heart at the thought that they wanted to get anywhere with her, had tentatively spilled some cherished anecdote of childhood sadness, would begin to uncover the tip of her feelings of loss and sorrow for her father's death. They would urge her to confess times when she had behaved badly, so she would dare to speak of the least appalling jealousies that affected her, like the feeling she harboured towards blonde girls and happy families. She would refer, at their demand, to times when she had felt fear and loathing, wondering as she spoke if this was what was meant by 'for better or worse'. But suddenly, she would overstep some invisible marker and the men would swing round and their listening poses, their wide open eyes and their inclined heads, would evaporate and they would stand up and move towards the door, saying, 'I'm sorry but I'm out of my depth, here.' And she could hear them thinking, 'You're weak, you're so weak. It's disgusting!'

She and men. They were always in each other's arms or at each other's throats, muddling along, nearly coming to blows. She could not quite believe that they did not love her more, because in part she thought she was probably the best thing that would ever happen to them, but when they decided to give her a piece of their mind, and hammered her into the ground with their harsh reckonings, she would generally listen at the other end of the phone, nodding, when she knew she should have just put the receiver down, saying, 'I deserve better than this.'

The tall man standing opposite at the party had looked quite normal when she'd examined him, he did not seem particularly anxious, or sad or ill at ease in any way. He was just a man, tall, dark and handsome, standing in a room at a party. But there was definitely something about him.

Good Love? Bad Love? said that attraction to men who had nothing to give was a pattern that stemmed from childhood and ought to be questioned. The women's magazines were the first to admit that the men with the hints and tints of tragedy were to be avoided. 'If he has more than two drinks before dinner, don't date him again. If he mentions his mother more than three times before dinner, don't date him again. If he smokes more than four cigarettes before dinner, don't . . .' And never put your eggs in the basket of a man who is sowing his wild oats.

But what if you weren't having any dinner, or if his mother was undergoing major surgery or he was having a particularly bad day? Or what if he had given up alcohol for Lent, say, and it was Eastertide. She knew, she had said a hundred times, with a note of cynicism that didn't belong to her, 'These men, these men.' But then, did you have to discount someone because he made a direct appeal to something inside you? Did the fact that you were drawn to a man guarantee him to be wholly unsuitable, if your instincts had proved unreliable in the past? Always? A woman might have a child to shield her from sadness, she might become absorbed in its sounds and gestures, losing herself in its world, and although this was bad luck on the baby's part, it didn't follow that no woman who was less than a hundred per cent happy should be allowed to conceive.

In life you were forever landing up against situations where you wished there was some sort of standard measure, some independent, advisory body you could apply to which would let you know when you were taking a calculated risk based on educated guesses, that is, when you were living life to the full (as you were meant to) or when, in a frenzy of poor judgement, you were throwing caution irrevocably to the wind. Any hungry fool could fall head over heels in love with a tall thirsty man with long limbs and big hands who called you Baby and looked after you if you pretended to be stupid enough not to do it for yourself. And you'd end up loving the wrong thing, hoping for the wrong thing, longing for something you didn't even really want. And the man would be happy, thinking that the best cure for a sad girl with fat tears in her eyes was kisses on tap. Anyone could do that with their eyes closed and their hands tied behind their back. But to turn away from good love made you just as culpable as choosing bad, didn't it? What if the man she was drawn to now was just a Normal Man? Maybe he drank a little too much, or worked a bit too hard, but maybe he was just a normal man with a big open heart with her name all over it. *Good Love? Bad Love?* said that hungry people make poor shoppers. But it only occurred to her to go shopping when her stomach was empty. She couldn't just write him off on the strength of some theory.

The path that lay between her and the normal man was clearer now. People were edging towards the smell of hot pastry that was coming from the kitchen. The girl in pink said, 'Let's pig out,' to the girl in green and they deserted the sofa for the kitchen. The music had stopped and the hostess, wearing a strappy leopard-print dress and sheer cream tights, turned over the record of Frank Sinatra's greatest hits. She lit a cigarette. She looked stressed and flushed, anxiously surveying the carpet for wine stains, red-and-yellow drum of salt in hand. She looked wearily at Janey and Janey heard her think, 'Why have all these people come to mess up my lovely new flat?'

'Can I help at all with anything, Lucy?' Janey said.

The hostess's eyes brightened, she gathered herself up into perfect hostess material. 'Thank you so much. It's all taken care of, so you see helping wouldn't be helping.' She beamed at Janey. 'I've been meaning to tell you, you're looking fantastic, you really are. What a transformation! How much weight have you lost? I wish I could lose a few pounds.'

Janey did not answer. More people were arriving, you could see them walking up the street, women running their fingers through their hair or hitching up their tights, men striding purposefully, checking doors for the right number.

'I don't know what's happened to the others from

college,' Lucy said distractedly. 'I hope they turn up. Shall I introduce you to some people?'

'Oh no, I'm fine,' Janey answered and the hostess slipped off into the kitchen. The curtains of the house opposite were drawn and the lights had gone out in all but the first-floor front room. Janey imagined the family going to bed, children upstairs at the top and mum and dad in the large first-floor front room with the two windows. It would be the room directly above the one she was standing in. The curtains were cream and threw a buttery light onto the street. They were probably having a kiss good-night now. Then the light went out.

Janey returned to the sofa. It was quite amusing knowing absolutely no one at all because there was no one to think it strange. She fixed her glance on the normal man's shoes. They were old brown lace-ups, scuffed in places, but shiny round the toes as if they had been polished in a hurry. The laces were loosely tied. The shoes seemed to indicate a relaxed, easy-going . . . but just then the left shoe lifted itself off the carpet a little and came down about four inches later. The heel of the right shoe raised itself off the ground but the ball of the normal man's right foot remained on the carpet. He transferred his weight back onto the right foot. A man who does not know how to walk, thought Janey clicking her tongue and raising her eyes to the ceiling, but as she lowered them again she noticed that the man's fancy footwork had a reason. The girl with the pink dress and the blonde hair was speaking to him, chest arched upwards and arms hanging slackly down. She must be wearing a push-up bra. Sinatra was singing, 'And then I go and spoil it all by saying something stupid like I love you.' Janey fixed her eyes on her own feet in her best black patent high-heels, bought a size too big for her in the sales (70% off) so that she felt like a child dressed up in her mother's things whenever she wore them. The man's old brown shoes were on the move now. It seemed more than likely that they were walking towards her. She must stop looking at them, make eye contact with him, give that all important first impression, smile, quick, pull a face, tell a joke, give a look, anything to make him sit down next to her. To lock eyes with a stranger, smile and then walk by is called a three-second love affair in America, she remembered hearing on some talk show. She raised her head to find him looking at her eyes. She stood up, holding her empty glass in her left hand.

'All right?' she said to him.

'You look very thoughtful.'

'That's the kind of girl I am,' she said. And then, 'It's a lovely party, isn't it?'

He didn't say anything. She put her glass down on the floor and made a small gesture towards the hostess, 'She doesn't seem to be having much of a time, though.'

'She's fine,' the normal man seemed sure. 'She likes doing the hostess bit.'

'I like your shoes,' said Janey, grinning. (A man likes to be complimented just as you do.)

'They speak highly of you,' he said, returning her grin.

41

'I'm Janey,' she said and took a sip from his tumbler of whisky.

'You drink whisky like you're kissing the glass,' he told her.

'Is that bad?' she asked.

'No, it's good.'

'Good,' she said. And then neither of them said anything for a while. It was hard to know what to say. Say anything. Then to her horror she found herself saying, 'Would you like to hear a poem I wrote when I was four?'

'I'd love to,' said the normal man.

'OK, it's called "Nobody's Children".'

'Go on, then.'

'OK. "Nobody's Children".' She coughed.

'A mother and father died
And left the children five
They never got remembered
They never got forgot
They never got hungry
They had a magic pot.'

The normal man laughed. 'That's one of the best poems I've ever heard,' he said.

'Isn't it.'

'Shall we sit down?' the normal man said, slipping onto the sofa where the blonde girl had left her shiny black bag. It matched Janey's shoes. Janey moved it to one side, thinking, 'I really like this man.' She felt faintly sick in her stomach, but the man just seemed to her to let the moment carry him along without minding anything much. He was enjoying her company but only in an ordinary way. She sat down, allowing about eighteen inches between them. But the depth and the low height of the sofa and its many luxurious cushions threw them together. His eyes were pale blue. Janey straightened herself, tugged at the frayed hem of her skirt so that it approached her knees and tucked a stray curtain of hair behind her ear.

'You're thinking again,' he told her, and suddenly she shivered and he said, 'You're cold.'

'It's just my nerves,' she said.

'Your nerves are cold,' he said. He took off his jacket and she leant forward to let him put it over her shoulders so that she had four arms: perhaps he does like me after all, she thought. But seeing the ghost arms of the coat and feeling it still warm made her sad. Once she had walked past a house as a fat fifteen-year-old and seen a really handsome man waving to her again and again from an upstairs window; feeling very happy, she had waved back for several moments, joyful in his admiration of her, imagining a date they might go on, a life they might share together, until, vastly embarrassed, she realised that he had a violet tin of Windolene in his hand and hadn't been waving to her at all.

She cast her eyes round the room. Most of the people had gone through to the kitchen or spilled out into the back garden. Neither of them said anything for a while.

At last he spoke. 'It's so good being with someone

who understands silence.'

There was no answering that. She shivered again, but it was not the cold that she was feeling. She removed his jacket and laid it across her legs, then she cradled it in her arms so that it covered some of her upper body also. She lowered her eyes to her feet.

'Your shoes are like little boats,' he said, all smilingly.

There was something growing between them, there must be. She was having a feeling. She couldn't think what else to call it. The feeling was of something strange like inloveness. But you've only known him five minutes, she thought. She was probably just missing the actor, or perhaps it was only general longing. Maybe she had just parcelled up all the longing that was in her and stuck the name of this tall man on it, and she didn't even know his name. That's it, she thought. She felt something aching at the back of her eye: a lash that had got stuck, or was it a tear? She crossed her fingers. The man was wielding a certain power over her now. She wanted to be sick. 'Good Love doesn't make you ache, shake, feel sick . . .' She had not eaten anything all day, it might be that. It was easy to think it was your behaviour, your nerves that made you feel unwell, when it might be your waistband was too tight or you had swallowed your dinner too quickly.

The normal man was looking at her face 'All right?' he said to her as if to say, 'Be all right.' The girl with blonde hair returned from the kitchen to reclaim her handbag. Her hair was so fair and fine and soft and her skin was so peachy pink that she really did look like a

baby. She even smelled faintly of powderiness. Janey
arched her back to release the bag that she was sitting
on and gave it to her sadly. It's all very well going round
life being lovely all over the place but where does that
leave people like me?

People like me. Now she and the normal man were
looking straight at each other. 'Help me,' Janey
thought that he had seemed to hear her say, but all he
said was, 'Can I get you a drink?'

'Actually, I might just get myself one,' she said,
heaving herself up from the sofa. She had to get away
from him for a minute, even though she knew the Baby
Girl would slip into her place. The kitchen was lit by
white candles which had been positioned round the
room in pale blue saucers. The room was full of food.
The smell of it slapped you in the face. There was a
plate of red food, great glistening slices of tomato with
little green leaves strewn across them and a tray of
yellow and brown food, little mushroom tarts that
smelled sweetly of onion and garlic and ginger. There
was a pale wooden board covered with thick slices of
white bread and another board with a tall Stilton on it.
On the table sat a bowl of black grapes and a shiny pile
of cutlery and a large oval dish supporting a huge pink
fish with green and yellow twists of cucumber and
lemon decorating it.

Green and yellow, green and yellow,
Mother come quick cos I'm feeling quite sick
And I want to lay down and die.

The plates rotated before her eyes so that she was looking at five softly focussed pools of colour. The food kaleidoscope dizzied her and she gripped onto the table. It was over twenty-four hours since she had eaten anything. She picked up a large silver serving spoon and looked at her reflection in the back of it. She sighed at the sight of her face at once squashed and elongated. 'Bloody ugly cow,' she said under her breath. She folded a lock of brown hair behind her ear and tugged at her stretchy blue velvet skirt that had ridden up her thighs. 'I'm sorry,' she said to the face in the spoon.

She sat down by the table, stretched out her legs and put her feet up on another chair. A man breezed into the room and stopped. 'Great legs,' he said. 'Thanks.' But she was thinking about the normal man. He'd looked so tender when he said her shoes were like little boats. She should have made some joke about having sea legs or something. And now she'd probably lost him to Flossie or Mimi or whatever her name was. She took her feet down and tucked them under the chair. There were some green bottles of sparkling wine on the table, shimmering in the candlelight, and she took one and poured out a glass. She put her ear to the pale golden liquid to hear the sound of the bubbles fizzing, or the sea. A few stray strands of her hair fell into the drink. She squeezed them dry with her hands and she poured out another glass of wine, half hoping that the normal man would come and claim her. She waited impatiently, jabbing at some wax with the end of a spoon. Why doesn't he come? She pressed a finger into the warmed wax that lay beneath the wick and made a small channel with the edge of her thumbnail so that the hot molten liquid ran down into the saucer where it began to harden. Janey scooped out some of the warm wax and rolled it into small beads. She liked playing with wax even though it got inside your nails and on your clothes and slightly altered the feel of your palms. She had collected a large pile of white wax chips when the normal man came into the room and took a seat at her side. He began playing with the wax also. He took a credit card from his wallet and used it to shape the bits of wax into a picture. It was a face he was making. He pushed and slid the chips deftly, using cutting movements with some precision.

He stopped. 'Guess who?' he said.

Janey couldn't tell who it was meant to be.

'I don't know either,' said the man. He gave her a plastic card with a minicab firm's number on it and together they made a picture of a ballet dancer and then a chair, pushing the tiny pellets of wax to and fro. He was very good at it. They tried to make a picture of Diana Ross. And then he got up and went to the sink, took a large glass bowl from the draining board, filled it with water and returned to the table. He picked up a candle saucer which was brimming with molten wax and tipped it from a height into the water. Hitting the liquid the wax sank and then rose to form a long narrow milky ribbon which he fished out and divided into three sections of different lengths. The longest he made into a necklace and placed over Janey's head as if awarding her some sort of prize. The middle-sized strip he wound round her right hand three or four times to make a bracelet and the smallest piece he wrapped round her right index finger to make a ring.

'I feel just like Elizabeth Taylor,' she said.

'Well, you don't look like her,' the normal man replied.

'I know I don't.'

He picked up another candle and held it up to her. 'She couldn't hold a candle to you,' he said.

'Got any more poems?' he asked her.

'Well, there's "Blindness" and "Help" and "A Dying Dove".'

'Go on then.'

'Which one?'

'"Blindness."'

'OK. "Blindness":

'You took the twinkle from my eye
The light that made things glow.
Blackness now is all I have
And all I ever will.
A blurry sight is coming through
A sparkle in my mind.
I think I've got my sight back
No more am I blind.'

'I do enjoy a miracle,' he said.

'I like that in a man,' she answered.

Janey felt something fall into her lap. The necklace, on hardening, had become brittle and broken in two.

'Look,' she said.

'That's not a very good sign.'

'Ah well, it's been nice,' she told him and he laughed.

'What have you been doing today?' she asked him.

'Oh nothing much. I'm on holiday at the moment. Let's see . . . I got up late and read the papers and watched an old film on the TV . . . oh and I went to the builder's merchants to get some wood because I was going to put some shelves up, but I forgot that it closes early on Friday afternoons.'

'DIY,' she said and smiled. They were silent again for a while.

'I'm just going to have a pee, I'll be back in a sec,' the normal man said and got up, leaving Janey sitting in the kitchen with enough food to feed an army. She surveyed it intently. It felt like a huge risk to be taking. She ought to go back into the other room before she caved in and ate it all.

She had decided to try to lose weight a few months earlier, following an outing to a department store to find something new to wear. A trim assistant had shown her into a large, brightly lit changing room with a canny arrangement of mirrors which allowed you to see yourself from every angle. In an ambitious attempt to get into a size L blue linen skirt she had breathed in and tugged hard at the straining blue zip, managing to do up the first inch or two, before admitting defeat. Then she caught sight of the dimpled bulk of swollen pink flesh, squashed together in her attempt to contain it in the garment. She looked closely at her hips, now reddened with little teeth marks from the zip, and she saw the curdled fat protruding way beyond the possibilities of the fastening; it had made her gag. The assistant had returned to find her in floods of tears. The zip had broken and the sorry garment, stitches strained at both seams, lay in a crumpled heap on the floor, misshapen and useless.

'Not to worry, love. They come up really small, these French sizes. It's not your fault. It's shoddy workmanship. We'll send it back to the manufacturers.' She placed a hand on Janey's shoulder, but Janey flinched; she thanked the woman, apologised again and made her way swiftly to the exit.

The girls at school had been obsessed with weight loss: endlessly totting up their calorie intake, stealing their mother's slimming pills, daring each other to cut off and swallow their cardigan buttons to bring up their school dinner. Janey had remained aloof from these sharp practices which struck her as small-minded and immature. There was a certain meanness in such committed preoccupation with the appearance. Finally, Janey disapproved of such behaviour, but she did envy the intimate scribblings and whisperings of these girls, their high-spirited collusion, their common enemy.

The night of the incident in the fitting room, Janey worked herself up into the sort of hysterical determination that she had watched with mixed feelings at school. The sudden, tangible hardening of her will against weakness caused a surge of adrenalin in her, and, hand shaking as it wrote, she urged herself into the most unforgiving regime she could imagine: No sugar, No fat, No potatoes, No bread, No pasta, No flour, No rice, No meat, No nuts, No cheese, No eggs. At the top of the list she had written 'Copyright The March Miracle Diet'; at the bottom she had written 'I swear to stick to this diet, signed Janey March.' She had stuck to this (almost) every day for a hundred days and she had lost three stone, drinking vast amounts of tea and Diet Cola, eating fruit and salad, some Ryvita, lots of spinach and a small pot of yoghurt every day. This she supplemented with zinc and complex Vitamin B tablets. Now she was exactly at the recommended healthy weight for a medium-build person of her height.

A man entered the room and said in an Irish accent, 'I'm so hungry, I could eat a scabby horse.'

'I'm afraid the scabby horse is off today, Sir,' she said.

'You're a friend of Edward's, aren't you?' he asked.

'Edward?'

'You know, the guy you were just talking to a minute ago.'

'Met him here tonight,' Janey said.

'Like that, eh?'

'Like what?'

'You know, girl meets boy, boy meets girl. True life romance. Floral curtains, kissing, roast dinners, black and white movies, misunderstandings, vicious arguments, tearful farewells.'

She laughed. 'Who knows.' She put her hand to her head and waggled her lobe. 'Play it by ear,' she said.

'Have you seen the cake in the fridge?' the scabby horseman asked her, and he opened the fridge door to reveal an enormous cake covered in white icing with pink scalloped edging and white sugar roses all over it.

'Just look at that sugarcraft,' he said.

She had forgotten that that was the proper name for it. 'It's beautiful.' She decided to go and find the normal man. She was missing him a bit. She poured him out a glass of wine and went to the double doors. She looked over at the sofa but he was not there. Gone. But he hadn't gone, he was talking to a tall woman with dark hair now. They stood together by the other sofa; he had his back to the double doors. Janey stood at the boundary between kitchen and sitting room, wishing that he would turn round and call her over. The dark-haired woman was talking very quickly and smiling big fat smiles towards him. When Janey saw her brush his arm with her hand to make her point she took courage and decided to bring his drink to him, making a few steps in his direction, but still he hadn't turned round and she was only a couple of feet behind him now. To make her presence felt she stuck out a trembly wrist in order to hand him his glass from behind but just at that moment, to convey his point of view, the normal man threw out his right hand to the side of him in an extravagant gesture of emphasis, knocking hard against the proffered glass. Its contents leapt into the air. So alarmed was Janey at the suddenness of this contact that as she took the knock she gripped the glass as tightly as possible and it splintered and crumbled in her hand, biting into her arm. In an instant she pictured herself looking back at this event in time to come and murmuring, 'That was the first wound he ever gave me.'

But the normal man was marvellous in a crisis, deftly removing all visible trace of glass from her and wrapping up her arm in a big white linen handkerchief that was stiff and smelled of starch. He sent the girl in pink upstairs to fetch a towel which he wrapped around the handkerchief which by now was sodden with blood. 'Keep your arm raised,' he said, 'like the Statue of Liberty, to help the blood clot.'

Her arm was throbbing. It felt as if bits of glass were wriggling around inside her like tadpoles, stopping the blood from getting out. But there was blood seeping through the towel and onto her legs and on her face there were smears of blood from when she had tried to flick her hair out of her eyes. She was trying hard not to soil the new carpet or the furniture in any way, so she did not move her feet, and tried to confine all the blood to her body by catching any stray drips with her right hand before they could fall from her skirt down her leg and onto the ground, but it was not easy, there was blood in her shoes, warm and trickly. Keeping her arm elevated was a strain so she supported her left elbow with her right hand, feeling that she must look rather camp in her hour of need. She could smell the blood now, mixed in with the wine which she could feel damp on her shirt, and there were bits of wax everywhere. She smiled up at the normal man like a child not knowing what to do.

And then he was driving her to Casualty, through the traffic and the light summer rain, just to get a few stitches put in, he said, to be on the safe side. Her thin blood ran down her raised forearm, onto her leg and the car seat and fell in slow drips onto the floor, making little shiny puddles; she tried to mop them up with her good hand and the tails of the towel but it was impossible. The man tried to reassure and soothe and comfort her as well as a stranger could. 'I'm so sorry,' he said.

'But it was my fault,' she said. 'I don't know my own strength.' She clenched the fist of her good hand and bent her arm against itself so that you could just see a trace of bluish muscle standing out from beneath the short stretch-velvet sleeve. 'I go swimming three times a week. Mondays, Wednesdays and Fridays.' She hoped he was picturing her choppy little four-beat crawl. It was not exactly true, she had gone for some time on those days, but recently, for no apparent reason, she had stopped.

'It's just one of those things. You're very brave,' he said. 'We'll be there in no time.' Small tears were settling on her cheeks and chin. He talked to her in the voice that she sometimes used to speak to herself when she felt unhappy. 'It's all right. We're nearly there. Don't worry, everything's going to be all right. You've just had a bad shock.' She wanted him to say 'little one' or something like that to her, like the men who let you kiss them when you were crying.

'I hope you don't think . . .' she began, but she couldn't put words to what it was she didn't want him to think, or at least she didn't know what not to say. All she said was, 'I hope you don't think this is anything funny. If you've got to be somewhere, I can get a taxi, for the rest of the way,' she said.

'Soon be there.' The man ignored her words and instead he watched her eyes close as he stopped at the traffic lights. He listened to the sound of her breath. They were going through this together.

'Do you mind if I sing something?' Janey asked.

'Please do, that would be lovely,' said the normal man.

> 'I've lost my pal he's the best in all the town
> But don't you think 'im dead because he ain't.'

The man seemed to be giving her singing his best attention.

> 'But since he's wed 'e 'as 'ad to knuckle dahn
> It's enough to wex the temper of a saint.'

And here he laughed.

> 'He's a brewer's draymen with a leg of mutton fist.
> As strong as a bullock or an 'orse.
> But in 'er 'arms 'e's like a little kid
> O I wish as I could get 'em a divorce.

> 'It's a great big shame and if she belonged to me
> I'd let her know who's who,
> Naggin' at a fella what is six foot three
> And 'er only four foot two.
> They 'adn't been married but a month or more
> When underneath 'er thumb goes Jim
> Isn't it a pity that the likes of 'er
> Can put upon the likes of 'im.'

'That was great,' he said. 'Where do you know it from?'

'Oh, my Dad taught me all the old songs.'

'Will you sing it again?'

They drew into the hospital and somehow he knew that you had to drive about two hundred yards into an annexe at the back of the main building to get to Casualty. She stopped singing. To go to a hospital with someone, she thought. In a funny way they were spending the night together. She could hear him reassuring her. 'It's a great big shame,' they sang. 'Don't worry. I'll look after you,' he said, which made her feel that it must be serious. She knew that she had lost a lot of blood because she could see it everywhere and she could smell it, warm and rich on the blue velvet of her skirt. She felt weak.

'I hope they don't think that I did it, that I cut myself on purpose.'

'They won't think that for a moment,' the normal man said, 'because I'll tell them exactly what happened.'

'I don't even know your name,' she said.

'Edward. Honestly, it's all going to be all right.'

'Edward what?'

'Edward Oxley.'

'Janey March,' she said. 'March like the month.'

'Well, Janey March like the month, I'm really glad I met you.' He laughed. Afterwards she thought it was odd that he had said that because if they hadn't met she might not be in this mess.

Chapter 3

Casualty, in the small hours of Saturday morning, had a faintly theatrical air. It smelled like a pub. The sound of wailing floated in and out of hearing. There were sombre-faced family groups; old men in weary-looking coats whose original colours were unimaginable; young couples; some shrieking babies and then several stray drunkards, sad, put-upon shadows of their former selves, limping, tearful and bloody around the eyes. One man in particular was providing a sort of entertainment for the captive audience, issuing at intervals a paranoid challenge to a police officer who seemed to be hanging about to chat up the nurses.

'Come on, Grandad, easy does it,' the policeman said, putting his arm firmly round the lost man to curtail an imminent, staggering lunge (and the threat of this movement had also caused the normal man to raise a protective arm across Janey's injury). The policeman escorted the man back to his seat for the third time and sat him down in the orange plastic chair. A young nurse rewarded this show of gentleness with a warm smile. She swiftly wrote some numbers onto a scrap of paper and pressed them into the officer's hand. 'I'll be in touch,' he whispered as he slipped away.

'Love finds the strangest places to blossom,' said Janey, then wished she hadn't.

It became increasingly clear that there was little or no chance of seeing a doctor before dawn. A strict hierarchy prevailed. When they approached the same nurse for help she informed them that there were three bypasses which had to take priority, but that she'd send another nurse along, when she could, to keep them going until the doctor came. There were only three doctors in Casualty, it being Saturday. Babies and old people took priority. Janey was simply not injured enough to gain attention.

'We should have done it properly,' she said.

'What's that supposed to mean?' the normal man asked. She did not answer. The man who had had the run-in with the police officer came up to them and said he needed 7p. While Janey fished the coins out of her bag with her good arm, the old man sat down next to her. He took a crumpled and frayed Christmas card from his pocket and showed it to them. An angel lolled in a champagne flute with holly in her hair and a tinsel halo. Inside was printed:

> Christmas comes but once a year
> Bringing hope and merry cheer,
> It's the time when God above
> Showers people with his love.

'Dear Dad' was written at the top. 'Love Sharon' was written at the bottom. He stood up after they had seen the card. 'She's got lovely writing,' Janey said.

The man beckoned to her with his hand. She moved her head slightly nearer towards him. He beckoned towards her again and scowled. 'I'd die for her,' he growled at them. And then he went off, smelling of alcohol and blood; Janey thought she probably did too. They waited for an hour and a half, watching and drinking tea from ribbed plastic cups which the normal man bought from a machine.

A family arrived in extreme distress. The mother was hysterical and her shrieks and screams filled the room. A nurse ushered her behind a screen. A younger woman, probably her daughter, carried on the shouting and anguished cries, and was shown behind the screen also. Janey shivered and the normal man took her good hand in his. The women's suffering must have been a match for that of the patient they had brought in. Pain didn't come any worse than that. Suddenly they were being treated like royalty. A tray with tea in green china cups and a saucer of shortcake was taken behind the screen, and after a short while they were led up a corridor and shown into a little room. It must be where you were taken to be told that the patient was dying. The last time Janey had been in hospital was when she had lost her father. There had not been any little rooms then, not as far as she could remember.

Everything was being done for this family. There was

almost something religious about the whole affair. The staff on duty were trying to ease the trauma, as if they had some idea that it might help if afterwards it could be said, 'But they were wonderful at the hospital.'

'There's no one here with anything funny stuck on their head, like a chamberpot,' said Janey, 'or a hand that won't come out of a tin can.'

'This isn't a *Carry On* film, you know,' the normal man laughed.

'My dad was in some of the *Carry On* films,' Janey said.

'Was he really?' the normal man was impressed. 'What was his name?'

'Norman March.'

'March like the month?' the man said.

'That's it.' And just on cue a tiny nurse of a certain age, with an enormous bust and a shock of brittle blonde hair, appeared and flashed them a winning smile. She had come to dress the wound. 'If you'd come in an ambulance the men would have done it, instead of leaving you bleeding to death.' She laughed. 'I'm going to have to poke about a bit to see if there's any glass left in. It's going to hurt.' She took them behind the same screen that had housed the wailing women. The tray with the tea things had been left on a small table, the untouched biscuits, the half-drunk cups of tea. There were three chairs.

'You know the women who were here a minute ago . . . ?' Janey's voice trailed off.

'The son has just died,' the nurse said. 'Only twenty.

Car crash. He was on his way to see his girlfriend. She'll be crying for him tonight.'

I've a wee little sailor girl in old Portsmouth town
And tonight she will weep for me for me for me
And tonight she will weep for me.

When the normal man had cleared away the tea tray Janey put her arm on the table, in the fashion of an arm wrestler, as instructed by the nurse. Rosie Bartlett was the name on her badge. Staff nurse. Janey turned her head away so as not to see the wound. With the nurse's first application of a pointed metal instrument to the gashed skin the pain was so intense that she involuntarily pulled her arm away and the sharp metal point made a long narrow scratch on her arm. Janey cried out.

'Come on now,' said the nurse. 'Has to be done, I'm afraid. Be brave. Let's be having you.' The nurse sprayed something cold and yellow on Janey's arm. Janey looked in the opposite direction, straight at Edward. He was holding her hand and she was squeezing it hard.

He took deep breaths and told her how brave she was. 'You're doing so well,' he was saying. She took tense inward breaths and bit onto her lower lip. She sniffed back a drop of moisture from the end of her nose. The room smelled of scouring powder.

'Soon be over,' the normal man said. The nurse dressed the wound. She couldn't see what with, but it was an enormous relief, until she felt tape fastening the dressing, pulling sharply on her arm hair, as it was put into place. The normal man still held her hand. The relief that the nurse was no longer poking inside her had subsided a little, as the throbbing pain returned. A troubled heart was beating inside her arm. She looked at it. From her elbow to within an inch of the swollen tips of her fingers stretched a soft white wad of padded bandage. The nurse briskly attached a pinky brown foam rubber apparatus to the bandage, threading it round Janey's neck and across her body to the other side of the wound, so that a support was formed to ensure that the arm remained upright. Then she left them. Janey began to cry noiselessly and leant her head on the normal man's shoulder. The normal man carefully put his arm round her. 'Thank God I am not here on my own,' she thought. The last time she had been in hospital, when her father had had his heart attack in the street and died, was nearly ten years ago. In fact it was nearly ten years ago to the day, the anniversary being on 23 June, two days' time.

Another hour passed and another. She was tired and hot and her arm was hurting. The normal man still held her hand and told her bad jokes and funny stories at intervals. She hoped his staying with her was more than the sort of formal manners that made some men walk on the side of the pavement closest to the kerb. What was it they called it? Oh yes, Old World Charm. The nurse probably assumed they were a couple, out together at night in partyish clothes. Janey thought back to what might have been at the party, what could have happened next. Of course, she would not have gone home with him, not unless she was feeling really bad, but then she had not been feeling too good about things. He was certainly of the type of man that she liked. Tall, and tall to her meant six three or four (she was five eight herself), smiley, friendly, a bit mad. The expertise he had shown in getting her to the hospital had touched her. He had arranged it all so quickly; the towels and knowing about holding her arm erect seemed like some strange ancient love test in which he had certainly proved himself. But to someone else it might not look so good.

The nurse came back with a doctor to carry out some tests to see if she had lost any feeling in her fingers. The idea of not having any feelings! Once the three of them, Mum, Dad and Janey, had gone to the dentist's and the dentist had congratulated her on her perfect teeth and the fact that she didn't need to have any treatment. 'He says I've got no feelings,' she proudly announced to her parents and opened her mouth wide as they laughed and her father had corrected her pronunciation. But this was more serious. 'You look like you've lost your heart and found your shirt button' was an expression her father had occasionally used. It might be that she had bartered a limb for this man, although perhaps the man was much more than a shirt button. But then she had always been vain about her hands and wrists. They were particularly slender and elegant. They were the hands of a person of a build quite different from her own, or at least different from the large bulky frame she had inhabited until about three months ago, before the diet. If this was a film, she mused, as the doctor stuck needles of assorted lengths and widths into her, asking if it hurt and she could feel almost nothing, she would be a pianist, in the Joan Fontaine mould, repeating to herself over and over, 'I will never play again.'

The doctor, when he eventually returned, heard the story and said, 'What an unlucky accident.' They were trying to find her a bed so they could get some investigations done in the morning. They had to check if any tendons had been damaged. And there was another long wait. Janey told the normal man to go home; he said, 'No way, José.' She tried to fall asleep but she kept waking and not knowing where she was and at half past five she was given a bed, a hospital nightgown, a painkiller and a *Nil by mouth* sign. Helping her to undress the nurse told Janey to remove any jewellery and then, realising that Janey's right hand could not remove a ring from itself, she drew off a gold ring with a little pearl on it, a present from her father.

'I'll give it to your boyfriend to look after,' she said. Then there came a kiss goodnight on the cheek from the man and a promise that he would return in the morning, first thing.

Out of the blue she had received a message saying that he had collapsed in the street while she was in an English lesson – *Jane Eyre*. The school matron had taken her in a taxi to the hospital. Matron, with her coal-black hair and her reassuringly ugly face and squat figure, was still dressed in her second skin of bubblegum pink overall under her herringbone coat. They hadn't talked much. Matron had heard her sniff and said, 'I hope you're not getting that bug that's going around.'

At the hospital Janey had run down a long grey corridor with matron's shoes clacking behind her. At the end of the passage the figure of her mother was standing with her face to the wall; recognising her hair and her shoes and her coat from the back, Janey had shouted out, 'Mummmmmm,' and run towards the willowy form. Her mother swung round violently to face the child. Her face was as pale as flour. And then she let out a great scream. And with the scream Mrs March seemed first to crack, then split in two, then splinter into four, eight, sixteen smithereens and the grown woman's body crashed against the wall and fell in a heap on the floor.

That memory, the stuff that recurring dreams are made of (Janey was dreaming it now beneath the *Nil by mouth*), ought to have caused a bond between mother and daughter even as it was happening. The dreamer knew you should feel close to someone if you have gone through something as big as life and death together. But as soon as her mother had let out the scream Janey knew that she had intruded on something. That she shouldn't have come. She had done wrong; why had she been brought there? So she had stood very still, pressing her body against the wall, with her eyes firmly shut, trying not to be there as best she could. Over and over again the thought came to her that if she herself had met with an accident and died her father could have made sure her mother was all right. He knew how to handle her. These two people in the hospital (even now as they were given another chance to arrange things better by the dreaming head on the pillow) were at a loss as to how to help each other. A nurse arrived with some tea and Janey gave a cup to her mother, feeling at last that there was a way to be useful. Her mother thanked her.

'Was he in any pain?' Janey asked, with an idea that it was what you did ask. Her mother didn't answer.

After a while the nurse said, 'He died immediately. They did manage to revive him for a few minutes, but then he just slipped away. There was no pain.'

'I see.' And then Janey remembered poor Matron still lingering on the edge of the picture looking more lost than any of them.

'Is there anything else I can do, Mrs March?'

'You could take me back to school perhaps,' Janey answered.

'Yes, take the child back to school, please.'

When they got back to school Matron put Janey into the squat little white-wood bed in her office having given her a cup of hot milk into which she had dropped two Junior Disprin. The kind old woman gazed down at the young girl's sleeping head, long-gone golden hair covering the white pillow in little shining sworls, like an angel's. Beneath Janey's shut eyes the wide-awake child could hear the woman's muffled whispers as she prayed to the Father for the repose of the soul of Mr March, asked the Son to help Mrs March bear her sadness and turned to the Holy Spirit for the sake of the child.

Hail Mary, full of grace, the Lord is with thee. Blessed art thou amongst women and blessed is the fruit of thy womb, Jesus. Holy Mary, mother of God, pray for us sinners now and at the hour of our death. Amen. Hail Mary, full of grace, the Lord is with thee. Blessed art thou amongst women and blessed is the fruit of thy womb, Jesus. Holy Mary, mother of God, pray for us sinners now and at the hour of our death. Amen. Hail Mary, full of grace, the Lord is with thee. Blessed art thou amongst women and blessed is the fruit of thy womb, Jesus. Holy Mary, mother of God, pray for us sinners now and at the hour of our death. Amen.

Janey awoke to the sound of church bells ringing and the thump of her arm throbbing. One, two, three, four, five, six, seven, eight. A man was seated at the end of her bed. It was him. The normal man.

'How are you feeling?'

'Not too bad.' He had brought her some white stocks and he, or perhaps a nurse, had put them in a vase. 'Thanks for the flowers,' Janey said. In her family they were called apple pie flowers because of their spicy scent.

'I was thinking, would you like me to ring your parents or anyone, let them know where you are?'

'That's very kind. I don't think so, though. My mother's away till Monday and my father . . .' No more words came.

'All right, well, if you think of anyone, just say.'

'OK.'

'I'm starving,' Janey said. The normal man pointed towards the *Nil by mouth*. 'Couldn't I just have a bit of something? Couldn't you pop out and get me some chocolate?'

'Oh no you don't.'

'Whose side are you on?' she asked him. The normal man reached into a carrier bag and she saw to her delight that he drew out a copy of *Anna Karenina*. 'I thought you might like to have someone read to you.'

'That would be lovely.' She closed her eyes. 'It's one of my favourite books as well.'

'Here,' he said, and wrote down the initial letters w, y, t, m, i, c, n, b, d, t, m, n, o, t? These letters stood for, 'When you told me it could not be – did that mean never or then?' There seemed no likelihood that she would be able to decipher this complicated sequence; but he looked at her as though his life depended on her understanding the words.

She gazed up at him seriously, then leaned her puckered forehead on her hand and began to read. Once or twice she stole a look at him, as though asking, 'Is it what I think?' 'I know what it is,' she said, flushing a little.

Janey was drowsy and tearful. A woman would never

have chosen to read that bit, never arrive with a passage about a betrothal, when there was something funny going on anyway. (A man was allowed to say 'I love you' after a few days and the woman would be secretly pleased whilst reminding herself, 'It's just talk.' But if the woman said 'I love you' after a few days, well, the man would probably leave the country or something.)

It was beautiful though, that tentative written bond. But then Levin wasn't Kitty's first choice. Wasn't it better to have a terrible time with the man you really loved than a broken companionable time with someone who was good and kind? Or maybe, not then, because things were different for women, but maybe, now, you were better off on your own.

'How well I knew it would happen! I never dared hope, yet at the bottom of my heart I was always certain,' he said, 'I believe it was preordained.'

'And I!' she said. 'Even when . . .' She stopped and went on again, looking at him resolutely with those truthful eyes of hers . . . 'even when I drove my happiness from me. I never loved anyone except you, but I was carried away. I must ask you, can you forget it?'

The normal man stopped reading. In a tiny whisper he said, 'Are you asleep now?'

'No.'

'Shall I read some more?'

'Yes please.' And the normal man went on. Janey cried noiselessly into the pillow. Maybe she should ask him to contact the actor. But if someone dumps you and the next thing they know you are in hospital with a slit wrist . . . It would be humiliating. It might even count as emotional blackmail.

Why are you being so nice to me? Janey was asking the normal man in her head. In *Good Love? Bad Love?* there was a game you could play where your adult self, that is your competent, cheerful, lusty, tough side, sits in a chair and holds a conversation with your childish side, that is your dependent, unreasonable, grasping, needy self. Then you swap chairs so that the baby can answer the parent and then swap back again until you've said all you need to say.

Why are you being so nice to me, she asked the normal man in her head again.

Because I like you, she answered herself as the normal man might have done.

Why do you like me?

Because you're my cup of tea. She was dying for a cup of tea right now and one of the cakes she had made the day before for the man at the Dominion. It seemed like a lifetime away. She opened her eyes and focussed on the normal man. She hadn't been attending. Kitty and Levin were to be married.

> *Princess Shcherbatsky considered it out of the question for the wedding to take place before Lent, to which only five weeks remained, since half of the trousseau could not be ready by that time.*

A nurse stood at the end of the bed also listening to the

story, not wishing to interrupt. Janey could see her bob about and open her mouth and lift her head in an attempt to say something, but the normal man was too involved in the book to make her out, and as each sentence ended and she made as if to speak, another would begin until at last Janey caught the man's eye and gave a nod in the nurse's direction. The nurse stepped in and with some haste administered a painkiller to Janey with a 'Yes the doctor will be along at some point' and a 'No you can't have a cup of tea, I'm afraid.' Her business done, she lingered at the bedside to hear the man reading for a few moments, half absorbed and half distracted, her eyes darting about the ward for fear that she might be caught time-wasting. Janey looked at the man's face, his smiling eyes and his dark, untidy hair and at the nurse, with her blue and white uniform and neat features captivated by the sound of his voice, and her eyes filled with tears of pride. He had been reading for nearly an hour and she could hear his reading saying: I, L, Y, B, Y, M, C, O, T. These letters stood for 'I like you because you're my cup of tea.' He was looking at her now and when he saw the tears on her cheeks she was sure that his heart must be breaking for her trouble.

'You are in the wars, aren't you,' he said.

Janey liked people who had a good command of English idiom. Someone who would say, 'How are we off for time?' instead of 'What time is it?' She liked people who expressed disappointment and disapproval by saying, 'It didn't really cut the mustard' and 'Fine words butter no parsnips.' People who took things with a pinch of salt and didn't hold their breath at the end of the day. A bicycle had once knocked into her when she was on a zebra crossing and the lollipop man, slightly sheepish, had said to Mrs March, 'I think this calls for a takeaway, Mum,' and it had made her day. It wasn't to do with being clever, it was just a general lightness of spirit and an enjoyment of words. A desire to colour in thoughts and feelings so that they became more cheerful and festive. Some of the men in the fruit market said, 'He couldn't sell a black cat to a witch' about each other. And then there were the times when people got it wrong by mistake. Mrs Clarke, who had been their neighbour in Greenly Terrace, up in arms about the latest antics of the woman who ran the paper shop, would say in a tone of the deepest outrage, 'Madge Nesbitt ceases to amaze me.'

Janey's father had had a lovely turn of phrase. With him it came from having spent years in rep. in bad plays where people said to each other, 'You know, you have the air of lost wealth,' and in good kitchen-sink dramas where people said, 'Well, between you and me, he's no oil painting.' In the small parts he had played in the *Carry On* films, he had picked up at least fifty-seven ways of using the word 'sauce'. There was even a photograph of him standing next to the young Barbara Windsor, her lips pouting and her two steam-pudding breasts squashed together and winking at him from the top of a pink dress.

On one of their many father-and-daughter walks in

the park a middle-aged woman had come up to him, very prim and proper she was, with shoes that exactly matched her handbag, and said, 'Excuse me, but are you Norman March?' He gave her a long low nod, grandly. 'Well, Mr March, England has a lot to be ashamed of, for example unemployment and football hooligans.' She paused. 'But she can be proud of you!'

In the ten years before his death he had worked on and off at one of the few remaining music halls in the country, where as the chairman (Norman March, March like the Month – 'Damp and Miserable' the audience would shout back), it was part of his job to introduce the turns with long, alliterative chains of words: 'The mellifluous melodious musings of that most marvellous of musical magicians, your own, your very own, Miss Marion Gray' – although his were much better than that. He also loved puns and so did Janey.

'I had a nasty turn on the way to the theatre tonight, but you know what they say, the nasty turns of today are the star acts of tomorrow.'

This liking for wordplay did not mean that Mr March eschewed plain speaking. Although 'March like the Month' was his self-styled introduction, he was sometimes referred to as 'Norman March as Plain as the Hair on your Head'. As Plain as the Hair on your Head, in his act, amounted to a dramatised criticism of his own appearance (his hair was thinning on top). Offstage, however, it was a significant pointer to his respect for sincerity, straightforwardness and truth. He

73

was made uneasy by any sort of double-dealing, any artifice offstage, in what he termed 'real life'. As a result of this, few of his friends were actors, a people whom he considered an occupational hazard. What he hated most about actors was their relentless use of charm. Once or twice in her lifetime, Janey, singly or with her mother, had been issued with a little speech on the subject in words to this effect: 'If someone is being charming, then nine times out of ten you can be sure that some funny underhandness is at play. Proper people with thoughts and feelings, wholesome and good people, wouldn't be seen dead exercising charm.' He spat out the 'ch' as if it were a bad taste in his mouth. 'Certainly, it can be a profitable way of going about things, but ultimately it brings humiliation to the victim because it exploits weakness through manipulation and it's harmful to the user because it is a refined form of bullying and as such it is bad for the soul. I do not say that it is not sometimes alluring because, without doubt, it is, but we have to teach ourselves to resist it in all its forms.'

For years, even now, Janey would catch herself, often in mid conversation, feeling particularly won over by someone, and grow alarmed at the thought that the person concerned might be doing it to her, this thing that was so low. But it was hard to judge when a person was being just plain lovely: kind, interesting, funny, attentive, or when there was a sinister element involved; when there was a possibility that a plan had been hatched, that machineries and consequences had been plotted and set in motion and every honeyed word was luring you closer and closer to the rocks which would wreck your ship.

Everyone said she had lost her looks the last few days, and on her wedding day she was nothing like so pretty as usual; but Levin did not find it so. He looked at her hair dressed high beneath the long veil and white flowers, at the high stand-up scalloped collar that in such a maidenly fashion hid her long neck at the sides and just showed it a little in front, and at her strikingly slender waist, and it seemed to him she was more beautiful than ever . . .

Janey had now and then thought about her own wedding dress and decided upon a simple shift made of white satin onto which, moments before the ceremony, white roses would be stapled with special white staples until the dress was completely covered with none of the fabric showing through. Then, as the day wore on, she would leave a trail of petals wherever she went, even up the aisle; the bridesmaids could pick them up and use them for confetti.

The normal man continued. It was extraordinary that he had been reading for so long. The word had spread amongst the nurses and from time to time a different one would appear and casually busy herself about some non-existent nearby task in order to hear the story. And so the cabinet next to the empty bed on Janey's right was wiped down and cleaned out several times and the blankets were smoothed down again and again. The water that Janey's stocks were in was changed and she was offered another painkiller minutes after her first which responsibly (she thought) she declined. Seeing the nurses so intent upon the reading, she was made less uneasy by the straying of her mind onto other things.

She hated hospitals. To her they spelt death, especially now, with the anniversary hanging over her. It was no place to spend a Saturday.

When her father was alive Janey had spent most Saturday nights with her mother at the music hall in the ugly modern building in a new development round the back of Charing Cross. Inside everything was pink: the walls, the chairs, the carpet and the curtains, the bar and above all the powdered faces of the artistes who lingered in the bar room before the show, huddled in front of the romantic Paris roof-top scene which hung there.

Generations of odours of sweat and paint and powder and musty costumes and broken-hearted cheeriness and missed warbled notes and knowing man-to-man looks would no doubt one day be absorbed into the walls of the theatre, fading the velvet curtains where the folds came and making the tautened velour seat covers discoloured and threadbare. For the moment, however, the atmosphere of recent development was inescapable. Everything was new. It was all made to last from quality materials so that in time it would distress to the artistes' satisfaction, but it would not happen overnight. Mr March would come home, full of how all concerned were attempting to speed the process of decay that would build character into their work place, and the cavalier attitude that was visible in their treatment of their surroundings.

They were none of them over-careful, there were spillages and the scrapings of props against walls. Back-stage feuds were lent momentum by the company's desire for a theatre with history and tradition. However, it was easy to keep clean and it was warm, which was more than you could say for most theatres in the West End, and what it lacked in shabby grandeur was made up for in personalities which, because of their neutral environment, were necessarily larger than life. It did not surprise Janey now that all this had been lost on her as a child. The music hall had succeeded completely in convincing her of its genuine involvement with the past. On her first few visits she had exclaimed to her mother, 'Look, they're dressed like people from the olden days!' She began to develop a taste for old-fashioned clothes. Long dresses with white aprons over the top and lace petticoats showing at the bottom. Gipsy scarves and shawls, hats with silk flowers, baskets and birdcages, collarless shirts, bowler hats, stripey bathing suits with little legs to the knee and bathing caps to be worn by three members of the cast whilst wrestling with deck chairs at the beach and singing:

'Those girls, those girls, those lovely seaside girls.
All dimples, hats and curls, your head it simply

whirls.
They look all right, complexions pink and white,
Diamond rings and dainty feet, golden hair from
Regent Street,
Lace, grace and lots of face, those pretty little
seaside girls.'

It was all standard music-hall fare, slightly embarrassed at its inevitable lack of authenticity, like a brand new piece of Victorian furniture, but nonetheless priding itself on being as sturdy and attentive to detail as a good reproduction could be.

'Hello, dearies,' the front-of-house manager, Clifford, would say, swinging his narrow hips (snakey hips, he called them) as he daintily stepped towards them, dropping a kiss on the hand of Mrs March and blowing one to Janey. He would usually say, it was a funning joke between them, 'What a lovely dress! Is it new?' even though Janey always wore the same wine-coloured velvet dress with the white collar that her father had bought her. And once when she had answered him with 'Oh, this old thing!' he had looked her hard in the face and said, 'Janey March, you are a little girl the likes of which I have not seen for many years.'

As the audience slowly filtered in through the large double doors Clifford would embark on a vicious running commentary in a stage whisper just loud enough to reach his victims' ears. Woe betide any latecomers, anyone with a loud cough or heavy cold, any persons in unusual attire or any old man accompanied by a young lady, 'Brought your Grandpa out love, that's nice.'

Often he would have a joke for them. 'The other day the wife says to me, "Sometimes, dearest, when I'm down in the dumps I likes to get myself a new dress." "Mmmmmmmm," I says to her, "I did wonder where you got them all from."' Janey would add it to her repertoire of bad jokes which she would reel out on request. She enjoyed the fact that the feeble stories were funnier when told by a little girl and liked to see her audience wondering if she knew where the heart of the joke lay.

'I went to the doctor the other day and the doctor said to me: "Would you mind taking all your clothes off," and I said: "Shouldn't you take me out to dinner or something first?"' This was a joke that Janey remembered telling when she was about six; and then there was, 'A friend of mine comes back from his holiday with a lovely tan, all over from head to toe apart from on his whatsit. So he decides to get along to Brighton to top up his colour and he finds a beach and covers himself with pebbles leaving a straw at his mouth so that he can breathe and his whatsit showing. And he lays there for a couple of hours until his whatsit is done to a turn and then two old ladies come along and one says to the other: "'Ere, Mable, to think that fifty years ago we married for one of them, and now they're bleeding growing wild!"'

Clifford would tell them show business anecdotes in

the interval if Norman had to stay backstage. 'Did you know Cyd Charisse's legs were insured for a million pounds and Ken Dodd's teeth are insured for two million pounds?' he once asked them.

'Well, I know which I'd rather have,' said Janey.

Janey loved to lose herself in this world, it became her own. The boy she loved was up in the gallery, and she would raise her eyes and focus on a faraway face of long ago. She saw herself staggering outside the pub on a Saturday night as 'one of the ruins that Cromwell knocked about a bit'. She knew so many songs that they provided a sort of punctuation to her day. Once she had sat down with her mother and father to a plate of cornflakes in the morning and started singing a song that she didn't even know she knew: 'For breakfast I never thinks of 'aving tea, I likes my 'alf a pint of ale.'

This love of songs lent Janey's childhood an old-fashioned air. Although like the other girls at school she knew all the words to 'Tainted Love' when it was number one in the charts, she also knew all four verses of 'Are We To Part Like This, Bill?'. Indeed, to this day, she still hoped she might go out with a man named Bill and maybe things wouldn't work out too well between them, but if they did fall out she could sing to him, not perhaps all four verses, but just the chorus:

> Are we to part like this, Bill?
> Are we to part this way?
> Who's it to be? Her or me?
> Don't be afraid to say.

And if it's over between us
Don't ever pass me by.
You and me, friends should be
For the sake of days gone by.

(Only, knowing her bad luck, they'd probably fall head over heels and live happily ever after.)

At the music hall it had been sung by a woman whose ability to look absolutely heartbroken at the same time as seeming relatively cheerful and brave had earned her considerable renown. That was how Janey sang it too and it had really been quite comic, people said, coming from an eight-year-old, especially when she faithfully reproduced, on the final chorus, a knowing wink and a rustle of her skirts on 'for the sake of days gone by'. Life had taught the music-hall artiste – or at least had taught the character in which the music-hall artiste had sung the song (it was hard to remember there was a difference) – that happiness lies only in difficulties overcome. This was the morality of the music hall, really, and also that singing makes you feel good when you feel bad. And of course the idea that a little of what you fancy does you good was a notion even modern medical science would be hard-pressed to refute. These things were a gift to Janey from her father when he was alive, before she even really knew what they meant, and they were there for her as a legacy and a strategy when he died, etched on her heart as a sort of family motto from all the singing they had done together.

For a forty-nine-year-old heaving-breasted bottle-blonde actress, safe in the knowledge that she was the youngest and most glamorous member of the cast, 'Grin and bear it' was possibly some sort of equipment with which to meet life head on, but for an eleven-year-old child, suddenly bereft of her adored father, with an inconsolable mother to take care of, even a child with all the courage that it could muster, this legacy could only fall short of meeting her day-to-day expenses. When she sang 'Bill' after her father had died, it was impossible for her to sound anything other than heartbroken.

Soon after he had died Janey had bought a book with her pocket money called *The Family and Death* and she read it at nights under the bedclothes with a torch that her father had given her. In the privacy of her room she took to wearing his jumpers which came down to her knees; she rolled the sleeves up several times so that they made bizarre shapeless dresses that smelled and felt of him, soft warm cashmere on her arms and legs and neck and chest. It was the best cure-all, cashmere, he used to say, for misery, for a blinding hangover, lovesickness, disappointment, the flu; it let your body know you were feeling a bit sorry for yourself without you having to go on about it.

After a few days Janey started sleeping with her mother as her mother did not like to be in the great big bed all alone. They tessellated, the two bodies, the larger making a zigzag with her knees that formed a little alcove for the smaller pair of knees to slip into. The book said that the mourning process must not be repressed, so Janey did not try to stop herself from crying for him every day. Often, after school, when she had had her tea and before she had her supper, she would sit on the floor in her bedroom and draw her knees up to her chest, pulling his jumper down over them and tucking it under her toes and then she would sway and shiver as she looked at photos of him and even listen to his voice on the answerphone tape that she played on her own little cassette recorder. To shut her eyes and pretend that he would soon ring or soon come home to them and it had all been a silly mistake, a nightmare or a terrible practical joke was somehow easier in the lull between the two meals which made a comfortable sandwich of her grief.

'Hello All, I've got the night off tonight and I'm bringing home some fish for supper. Byeeee.' That was one of her favourites. She'd taped as many of the recordings of his voice as possible onto a single cassette so that she could listen to a history of him through his messages.

So she would have tea, tea and toast and honey or Marmite if there was any in, eating it on her own when she got back from school. Then she would go up to her room and have a cry over her homework. About seven thirty she would have supper with her mother. Gradually the teas became more drawn out. There was a large jam jar full of coins in the kitchen, which, since the death, Mrs March had made available to Janey in case she needed anything extra to cheer herself up. So sometimes she bought a date slice or a doughnut at the baker's on the way home to eat with her toast or a Mars bar which she would divide into ten pieces and have a bit every five minutes until it was all gone, in case it was too rich to eat all at once.

Sometimes she would cut up lots of vegetables and make a dip out of cream cheese and yoghurt and chives from the garden. Mr March had been a keen grower of herbs, and soon after he died Janey picked a great bundle of them and tied them up in little bunches with white cotton: rosemary, parsley, sorrel, thyme, mint, chives, sage and tarragon, and she arranged them to make a green border round the grave after they put the coffin in.

Sometimes she would cook a bowl of rice and eat it with butter and grated cheese. And by the time she had made it all and washed and dried and cleared away the plates and the mess, even though she often ate and washed up simultaneously, by the time she got upstairs to start her homework and have her cry, it was almost time to come down again. Then, after a year or so, she began to develop an interest in cooking, so that from time to time when her mother came down at half past six to see about some food Janey would be in an apron with flour in her hair, kneading dough, or with onions frying gently on the stove and *Italian Food* by Elizabeth David open on the kitchen table. Mrs March might come down at seven o'clock in her night clothes – she was tired all the time – to find her daughter topping and tailing, peeling, chopping and grating or ladling out stock at arm's length, leaning away to avoid the steam. And they would have splendid dinners together that the mother would eat gratefully and the daughter would dish up with pride: hot food, rich in flavour, high in protein, always more than enough, with home-made bread, hard-crusted with melting insides, and pudding, crumble, hot lemon soufflé from Robert Carrier, chocolate cake which soothed them both, calming their nerves, tranquillising their waking hours and helping them sleep.

Janey continued to wear her father's jumpers. There were three of them, navy, camel, and dark red, and an inch of the bottle-green pleats of her school uniform skirt just peeped out below. While she cooked and while she ate she protected her father's jumpers with an apron to keep them safe. And all the while Norman March lay inside her stomach waving and calling to her and all she could do was to bury his cries under a small mountain of food, as if eating for two.

In her hospital bed with the arrangements for the Kitty–Levin marriage well under way, Janey embarked on some mental romatic calculations of her own.

Janey March loves Edward Oxley

LOVES
---

1 1 0 3 0
2 1 3 3

EIGHTY-ONE PER CENT COMPATIBILITY!!!!!!!

Nil by mouth. Janey was starving. Bacon sandwiches on brown bread that had been toasted on one side only. Mayonnaise, lettuce, tomato. Cup of tea. She had never wanted a cup of tea more in her life. Must be dependent, she thought. A plate of chips!

'Are you asleep now?' the man whispered again.

'No.' Her answer was weary. The painkillers had taken effect. She was losing all consciousness of the ward, the bustle of the nurses bringing round breakfast to the lucky ones, the occasional rattling of the medication trolley, visitors arriving and departing, sensibly nursey lace-ups treading spongily across hard floors. She had stopped taking it in. The movements were slow and soundless. It was story corner, wedding bells were ringing for Kitty and happy ever after. She was all tucked up in bed and a man she liked (81%!) was reading to her because she was in the wars.

'Are you asleep?' came the normal man's stage whisper and this time she was too tired to answer.

The next thing she knew, one of the little nurses was giving her a jab in the thigh and she was on a stretcher going down to theatre, chattering away to the porters. 'Don't take me to Birmingham instead of Crewe, I mean Crewe instead of Birmingham,' she said, feeling foolish. And the next thing was the doctor standing over her.

'You've been very lucky indeed,' he told her. 'You were a millimetre away from severing an important nerve, but no permanent damage has been done. Your arm should heal completely in two to three months but you'll have to keep it in plaster for the first five weeks. You can go home this evening. Please arrange for someone to collect you.'

As if by magic, 'Let me drive you home,' was what the normal man said when he returned later that evening.

Chapter 4

Janey had been living in a flat on the top floor of a luxury mansion block off Victoria Street for eighteen months. A polished mahogany banister and oatmeal-carpeted stairs or an oak-panelled lift that held up to four people in its masculine interior took you up to it. The flat had belonged to her father's dead aunt and it was filled with the dead aunt's things: her light blue and white plates, her teacups, her lacy mats and checked cloths and covers that bore the signs of years of careful starching and ironing. They were a little melancholy, her things, but they also had a freshness to them that put you in mind of the seaside. In the kitchen there was a row of sky-blue enamel storage jars with white upper-case lettering: SUGAR, RICE, FLOUR, BEANS, OATS, RAISINS, TEA, COFFEE, and an old round table on which someone had stuck a sky-blue and white gingham formica top. In the sitting room, a room which, by all accounts, the woman never used, with its fine high ceiling, its floral mouldings, its three long windows and its chandelier, there stood three chairs upholstered in faded willow patterned fabric with pale wooden legs and wood-tipped armrests. On the circular back of the middle chair only the horizontal threads of the material remained, some taut and some drooping like half-finished darning. There was a hole in the seat where the stuffing peeped through. A square mahogany tea table was set against one wall, a small book slotted under its shorter back leg. The poems of Robert Burns. Over the fireplace there was a mantel-piece on which ornaments had been arranged – a porcelain figure of a timid-looking flower-seller, some greetings cards, a snowstorm paperweight with scenes of Scottish heather inside it, a white china basket covered with tiny violets, once filled with toffees (they were all eaten now), a miniature straw sombrero, a wooden clog ashtray with tulips on it, and a pair of little silver ballet shoes on a blue velvet ribbon. Then there was a plain postcard on which someone had written, in much looped writing under the words 'the address only to be written on this side':

> So I says to meself, though you may be on the shelf
> Never mind Mary Anne, don't care
> For there's lots of tunes to play on old fiddles
>   so they say
> So I lives in 'ope if I dies in despair.

On each side of the hearth there was an armchair upholstered in heavy yellow-white damask. Each had antimacassars and sleeves fashioned from newer pieces of the same fabric and these were thicker, fresher and more densely patterned than the material on the main body of the chairs. At the windows hung heavy cream and blue patterned silk curtains. They had been arranged so as not to reveal their torn lining and many frays and were never drawn in deference to their fragility. Behind them were cream lace nets through which the sun shone, making floral patterns on the carpet in triplicate. The thin, pale carpet had a blue ribbon and bow motif border which also seemed emotional somehow, like night clothes. In Janey's bedroom and the spare room there were important French beds with wooden ends that curved and rolled over like scrolls.

'Do you think you could be happy here?' the dead aunt's distant cousin (they had none of them been able to work out exactly what relation he was to Janey) had asked her before his departure for a new life in Spain. He was said to be rather a self-dramatising sort of man. It was rumoured that he kept an envelope amongst his papers labelled 'In the event of my untimely death'. He too had played the halls in his time, specialising in a dazzling dramatic rendition, with many reddened lighting effects, of that old classic, 'The night I appeared as Macbeth'. (I acted so tragic, the house rose like magic, etc., etc.)

'I do, yes,' Janey had answered him.

There was a slightly theatrical clause to their arrangement. Mr Lord, for this was the name of the cousin, might occasionally ask for one of his friends to be put up in the flat; there would always be at least two days' notice, but it would mean having things ready at all times, just in case, he had told her. Janey rather fancied herself as a landlady: stern and intimidating but with a well-hidden heart of gold, got up in a floral housecoat and curlers, saying things like, 'The Very Idea!' and 'I don't know to what you're referring!' Or warm, indiscreet and bosomy, all shoulder to cry on and frilly pinny. But as yet these guests had never materialised. She made little concessions to them, like always having a boxed toothbrush and an unopened tube of Aquafresh ready and waiting. She had prepared an elaborate welcoming routine which involved a cream tea, well-chosen expressions like 'You look like you could do with a sit-down' and the airing of the spare bedroom, but as yet she had never been required to take any of this beyond the rehearsal stage.

Janey was all too aware that the flat was not by any stretch of the imagination a young person's dwelling. It exuded something of the atmosphere associated with distressed gentlefolk. It was strange for a person starting out in life to be surrounded by the trappings of reduced circumstances, as if she had somehow known better days, been the widow of some important MP (Churchill had lived in the block at one time), and had been left debts that she had only just been able to meet. Living in Musgrave Mansions lent Janey's life an old-fashioned air which she felt the need to counter by making sure she kept abreast of current events, new trends and products, the songs in the charts and the developments in the major soap operas. She would watch out for new lines that came on the market: transparent cola, jaffa cakes where the spongey bit in the middle was chocolate flavour or the topping was white, peanut butter and grape jelly in pretty dartboard stripes, liquorice-all-sorts ice cream tubs, calorie-free maple syrup imported from America. She tried to make her mark on the flat. She introduced some of her own things onto the mantelpiece. A tube of Rembrandt self-whitening toothpaste, a picture of Marie Lloyd, a postcard of Henry James, a Stevie Smith poem which she had copied out in her best handwriting on the back of an airmail envelope:

> What is she writing? Perhaps it will be good,
> The young girl laughs: 'I am in love.'
> But the older girl is serious: 'Not now, perhaps
>   later.'
> Still the young girl teases: 'What's the matter?
> To lose everything! A waste of time!'
> But now the older one is quite silent,
> Writing, writing, and perhaps it will be good.
> But really neither girl is a fool.

Janey was conscious that people might be reminded of an old lady on seeing her in the flat, so she would try to seem as little like one as possible, never knitting, clicking her tongue only rarely, not talking about the past or reading biographies, not wearing slippers. But the old songs from the halls or from the films, she couldn't give up. She loved to sing, to stop now would be, in the words of Mrs Clarke their neighbour in

Greenly Terrace, 'to cut off her nose despite her face'. Over the past few months it had been the sadder tunes she had found herself singing; shipwrecked loved ones, drunken mothers and abandoned children peopled her songs. But on a good day she might be heard singing 'I've got a lovely bunch of coconuts' in the bath, and she often burst into 'If it wasn't for the 'ouses in between,' whilst cooking in the kitchen.

The kitchen was the heart and the core of the flat because it was the only room that had heating Janey dared to use. Shortly after she had moved in the gas board had condemned all her appliances. The man took one look at the handsome boiler in the bathroom, gleaming white enamel, sparkling metal spout, top of the range in its day (but when that day had been, who could say?) and he shook his head.

'Like to live dangerously, do you, love?'

'Your problem is you live too far from the edge,' Janey mumbled under her breath. It was distressing to have the gasman stick great red warning triangles on both the Ascots and the gas fires, saying *Danger. Do not Use.*

'You want to get your dad to kit this place up properly.' He cast an amused eye round the flat. 'Place like this. You could make it really nice.'

So the oven in her kitchen warmed the room. She would light it in the morning (even in summer the room seemed chill without it), and turn the dial up to regulo five which was the highest it could go without jamming. And she continued to use the bath once a day, but always opening the window and the bathroom door before she got in which the gasman had told her, strictly off the record ('Don't quote me'), would probably see her all right. Janey solemnly signed the disclaimer saying she refused to have the gas supply switched off and would not sue the gas board if the wind changed and the carbon monoxide had her name on it. She couldn't anyhow, she pointed out to him, she'd be dead. She peeled the *Danger* sticker off the Ascot because it was disheartening to lie in the long and low bath and have it admonish her: superior, reproachful and wholly uncomprehending of the fact that she could not afford to replace the appliance. She didn't want to ask her mother for anything ever again and it seemed hardly fair to mention it to Mr Lord, considering he was letting her stay there rent-free.

The heat that the oven gave off was damp and sleepy. It sent small tears of moisture running down the walls and caused the windows to steam up. It was in this room that Janey did her college work on the formica-topped table, gazing out of the two windows which loomed down pleasantly over Westminster Cathedral. White curtains, printed with sailing ships in shades of blue and yellow, hung at each window and on the floor there was an expanse of deep-sea blue, marbled lino that was cold and slippery on her bare feet as she sat and wrote:

> *The response that Jane Austen's novels invite is at odds with what their writer reveals them to be. Jane Austen's*

narrative methods direct her readers almost immediately into an uncritical frame of mind, persuading us to part with something intellectual (perhaps the very desire that turns a reader into a critic), as we become absorbed in the characters and events she unfolds. Jane Austen defines a comfortable place for her readers which exists as a kind of critical haven sustaining the boundaries of her 'two inches of ivory' and repaying the author with almost complete freedom within that space. Jane Austen ensures that we allow the writing to absorb us to such an extent that any encounter we might have had with form is sacrificed for the sake of maximum involvement with the characters in whose world we are enclosed. We are prevented from seeing outside the structures that wall their actions. Her art depends on an insistence that we enjoy this surrender and we love what she requires from us: that we need neither look nor judge. We become unnoticing as we relax within her characteristic world, all longings sated by the feeling that we know absolutely where we are and want to be there because it feels like home. This response of child-like complacency prompts the simple, intimate and unliterary in us to seek out their mirror images in the writing. It also embraces our human desire for the knowledge of beginnings and endings that fiction promises.

'Men, like poets, rush "into the middest" *in medias res* when they are born, they also die "*in mediis rebus*" and to make sense of their span they need fictive concords with origins and ends such as give meanings to life and poems.'

But this response of absorption exists in its own right as

a created fiction as important and dynamic as any of Jane Austen's plots. Colouring all our readings and misreadings is the notion that we empirically exist in the interior of her novels. We jostle and function amongst her characters; we are implicated in their behaviours and misbehaviours. If we thought to withdraw from the writing we would find ourselves in a position which resembles looking at a group photograph in which we are included, standing in the middle but towards the back, fingers stained with strawberry juice from the fruit at Donwell or on one side of the narrow stage at Mansfield. Yet while we read we are made unconscious of this artificiality, of the fictitious nature of this response, because we are scarcely permitted to withdraw from the world of writing to experience it as art.

Janey entered the flat with the normal man in tow.

'What an amazing place,' he said. 'Do you live here all alone?'

'Yes.' She showed him into the kitchen, and they both sat down at the table.

'Shall I make some tea,' he asked, 'to settle you in? You should probably go to bed for a few days.' At last, the promise of a cup of tea. 'Could you get someone to come and stay with you?'

'I hope so, there's no food in the house.'

'Why don't I nip out and get you a couple of things, just to keep you going, in case you don't feel well enough to go out? Then at least there'd be something in the fridge.'

'I don't have a fridge.'

'Whatever, on the shelf then.'

Janey had once said to her tutor at college, 'I'm worried that my work isn't taking off,' and he had said, 'Don't worry, I'm sure it will and if not you can just be an ornament,' and she'd managed to come up with, 'What, and spend the rest of my life on the shelf!'

The normal man went out to find a food shop that was open on Saturday night without making her any tea. There wasn't any milk. There wasn't any tea. She gave him the key to let himself back in. Now that he was gone she found herself shivering. She changed into her night clothes carefully and decided to make a hot water bottle. That was one thing about the flat. It had a drawer containing five hot water bottles. She would make two. It had grown cold. Not cold for winter, but cold for summer suddenly. The normal man (bless him) had filled the kettle before realising that there was nothing to mix the hot water with and with the use of her good arm Janey managed to jam a matchbox between two cups and two books in order to steady it enough to get a light for the stove with one hand, laying the lit match just where the shoot of gas came out and then turning the knob. She lit the oven too. But when the kettle boiled it struck her that it was almost impossible to fill a hot water bottle with only the use of one arm. She sandwiched the bottle between her stomach in its white cotton nightdress and the kitchen sink and began to pour the water slowly in tiny trickles from the kettle which she grasped through a blue and white checked cloth. But she had put the ridged side of the bottle against the sink and as the bottle filled her stomach became increasingly hotter and little air bubbles interrupted the flow of the liquid and spat at her hand. Her stomach's grip on the bottle was loosening as it grew uncomfortably hot and her hand began to sting from the water bubbles. The bottle, almost full now, was slowly edging down towards her thighs, and the heavy enamel heat of the kettle was burning her hand through the cloth. She felt faint from the anaesthetic and the painkillers she had taken. Her eyes closed, and she forced them open: boiling liquid all over her abdomen would be more serious than her cut arm. Her eyes closed again. Put the kettle down, she said, put the kettle down, but it was too big and too hot, and the hot water bottle with its gaping mouth had slipped so that it was stretched across her, dribbling boiling water, then drops which were burning into her; she wanted to drop the kettle onto the floor but it would throw up boiling water against her and again her eyes closed; but this time the kettle was being taken out of her hand and the hot water bottle was having its stopper put in by the normal man and she wasn't too hot any more, and, when she opened her eyes, she couldn't stop crying. The normal man wrapped the bottle in the jumper that was tied around his waist and put it into her arms.

'For God's sake, what are you trying to do?'

'I don't know, I don't feel well,' she said.

'I think you should go to bed.'

'I know.'

It was time for him to leave now. He had arranged tea and milk and grapes and tomatoes and a lettuce and biscuits and cheese and bread in a row for her on the shelf above the kitchen sink, next to her recipe books. It was a long time since the last three foodstuffs had been in her life. She looked at the little row of goods.

'Thanks so much. There's no money in the house, but can I write you a cheque?'

'That's all right. It's the least I can do.'

'Are you sure?'

'Of course.'

'Edward?'

'What?'

'You're a really lovely person.'

'Thanks. You're not so bad yourself.'

'Thanks.'

'You going to be all right then?'

'Yep.'

'I suppose I'd better be off.'

'OK then.'

'Well, look after yourself.'

'I will.'

'I'm so sorry about all this.'

'Don't be. Anyway . . . What are you up to tonight?'

'I don't know, I thought I might watch the football.'

'When's that on?'

'In about half an hour.'

'Would you mind watching it here?'

'Have you got a telly?'

'Yeah, it's just through there.'

'Sure.'

'It's only black and white though.'

'That's OK.'

'The reception's not up to much either.'

'I'll sort it.'

Janey lay in bed and listened to the roar from the crowd, and the commentator's hysteria each time the possibility of a goal arose.

Norman March had liked to watch football on Sundays with a glass of something, after lunch. Sometimes Janey had watched it with him while her mother rested, a large Black Watch tartan blanket covering their knees. And she had gazed up at the reflection of the little men running around in her father's eyes as if they were two little portable TVs . . . or was that memory playing tricks on her? And all the while his whole face constantly shifted its expression: bleak, triumphant, at a loss, over the moon, sick as a parrot, wary, outraged, proud. (It was not for nothing he was on the stage.) It was exhausting just to look at him and she would make him a cup of tea or pour him out a drink, twisting her wrist into a little flourish as she finished pouring, like a waiter in a restaurant. They must have sat there like that for hours together, her eyes full of his eyes and his eyes full of forwards, his goalpost-mouth sipping from his cup or glass, the green and navy squares of blanket tucking them in cosily. She would smooth the blanket down every so often, or straighten it when the excitement of the game caused it to be dislodged, always making sure that it was slightly more over his legs than hers in the same way that her mother always gave him the largest slice of pie, the best cut of the joint, even if they had visitors. He was that sort of man. Everyone loved him and you always knew where to find him, because you just had to look for the centre of attention and there he would be, endlessly responsive to the demands of the moment. Norman March, March like the Month (Damp and Miserable – the cheek of it!), plain as the hair on your head, large as life, twice as beautiful, singing a song, 'I'm getting married to the widder next door', or 'I loved her and she might have been the 'appiest girl alive' or cracking a joke: 'The police were looking for a dangerous criminal, a dwarf clairvoyant who was wreaking havoc throughout the land. They combed the country high and low but couldn't find him anywhere. His criminal activities knew no bounds, the police became desperate, the country was up in arms, the Prime Minister, the monarch and the head of Scotland Yard held a meeting and as a last resort they launched a nationwide poster campaign: DANGER: SMALL MEDIUM AT LARGE.'

Well, it was funny when he told it. Janey told it at school, only she said Small Midget at Large without realising and there was no joke at all.

The normal man probably liked a joke, but then normal men do. Janey was bored of lying in bed. She got up and put on her dressing gown, looked at herself in the mirror and frowned. She looked a sight. Her face was a light shade of green. Her spot had taken on a whole new lease of life. Her hair was so greasy, it looked like she'd been out in the rain. 'Bloody ugly cow,' she said out loud, putting some mascara on her upper lashes, pinching her cheeks to try and get back something that might resemble a milkmaid complexion and slipping on some high heels over her socks; she went to join the man in the TV room. He was sitting on the floor with his legs outstretched, leaning back against a stack of newspapers which were piled into a knee-high tower against the wall. Janey lingered at the doorway.

'All right?' she said.

'What are you doing out of bed?'

'I wanted to see the match.'

'You like football?'

'I love it,' she said.

'Oh yeah?' He looked doubtful.

'No, really, I used to watch it with my Dad.'

She sat down against another pile of newspapers; they belonged to the flat and she felt it would have been wrong to have thrown them away. It was the commercial break. A happy couple reclined in front of an imitation log-effect, grinning after a hard day for her at the office and for him looking after the kids. Would that sell a mock traditional heating appliance though, she wondered? Adverts were mesmerising when you wanted everything. 'Are you a new man?' Janey was about to ask, but the game came back on. They sat and watched in silence. All the action was at one end of the pitch. She was just about to hatch a worry about the other goalie feeling lonely but she could not keep her eyes open and drifted off to sleep.

She awoke to the sound of music playing; it was half time. 'Da na na na na na na na na da na da na da na.' The normal man went into the kitchen and came back with a plate of bread and jam cut into triangles.

'I'm very impressed by your selection of jams,' he said.

'It's for when I have guests.'

'Like now, you mean.'

'Well, men come and stay the night sometimes.'

'Oh, I see.'

'No, I mean they don't actually come, but they might; friends of my landlord are meant to come and stay. Like a bed-and-breakfast sort of arrangement, in return for staying in the flat.'

'The jam's the breakfast then?'

'Men like jam, on the whole.'

'I'm sure, but they never appear, these men, these friends of your landlord.'

'No, but they might any day.'

'Oh,' said the normal man. 'How odd.'

They were talking even though the second half had started. Janey fell silent. SSShhh, her father had once hissed at her when she had spoken during play; she had never done it again because it had been one of the worst moments of her life. But just now she felt contented and even if it was only the painkillers talking and even though the floor was hard and her back and legs were aching as well as her arm, and it was cold, she could feel the warmth of a broad smile spread across her mouth. The normal man's eyes were on the screen. What would he do for his next trick? He'd practically cut her arm off, read her half the Russian classics, saved her from first-degree burns, bought out most of the twenty-four-hour shop for her. It was impossible to know what would happen. Janey fell asleep looking into his pupils for an answer.

When she woke it was dark, but the football was still on; different match though. The man was asleep. Janey got up and went into the kitchen. He should have had the left-over cakes for tea instead of the bread and jam. And he had done her dishes, which was no mean feat because there was no hot water in the kitchen since the gasman had insisted on dismantling her hot water heater until better ventilation was installed. She still had not eaten anything. It was thirty-six hours since she had had some Ryvita, two slices, dry, forty-eight cals. It did feel good when you could pull your stomach in so far that you didn't have one, but healthy living it wasn't. She turned off the oven.

It was nearly three weeks now since she had reached her target weight, but it was still rather alarming to look in the mirror and see that you were half the person that you used to be. She knew that her loss of three stone gave her something of the appearance of a normal-sized person, but she would often catch herself adopting or resorting to some of the characteristics of her fat self. She would edge her body forward cautiously, unsure of the extent of it, arranging her limbs in accordance with a sense of her own bulk, half knowing that it was with reference to a breadth and a mass of flesh which simply was not there to support these assumptions. And where had it gone, all that stuff, into thin air? Contaminating it with fatty gases as the carbon monoxide might contaminate her breathing air as she lay in the bath? Down the toilet? On the floor like sloughed-off skin cells? Was it just hovering over her, this dead flesh and fatty tissue, ready to pounce on her, if she relaxed for a second? Eighty-four packets of butter. With that you could build a little yellow playhouse or a waist-high wall. Sometimes on leaving the flat she would feel certain that she had forgotten something and would check her bag for keys, her essay, money, mascara, make sure she had not left a tap running, the oven on, the phone off the hook, and just when she had made sure that nothing was amiss she would glimpse herself in the mirror and realise that it was the fat that she had left behind. In a certain mood she felt naked without it, and she missed it (it had been so familiar, so completely what she was used to) in the way that it was possible to miss an old enemy.

She remembered how it had all started. One afternoon the other first-years in the playground were skipping with a long rope and singing skipping games.

> Rosy apple lemon tart,
> tell me the name of my sweet heart
> ABCDEFGHIJKLMNOP

Milkman milkman do your duty,
here comes Mrs Maccaruti.
She can do the can-can,
she can do the splits,
but most of all she likes to do the K-I-S-S.

She's fat, she's round,
you can bounce her on the ground,
Janey March, Janey March.
She's fat, she's round,
you can bounce her on the ground,
Janey March, Janey March.

'I'm not fat,' Janey said. And she looked down at her tummy and saw two little rolls of bottle-green woollen flesh peeping over the top of her pursebelt and she was genuinely surprised.

She'd go to the greengrocer's with her mother; one day the elderly woman who worked there handed Mrs March the bag of shopping with a sympathetic smile and said, 'Useless lump,' nodding at Janey. So they went to another shop but the young man who served them looked at Janey one day and shook his head. 'Oh, it's you,' he said, 'I thought there'd been a total eclipse of the sun! You've got to laugh.' So they removed their custom from that establishment too and found a new greengrocers and the man in the shop smiled at Janey and said, 'You're a nice big girl, aren't you love?' So they ended up buying fruit and veg at an Italian shop which was nearly twenty minutes away from where they lived and often the fruit was rotten and always it was overpriced but the man who ran the shop could not speak English and only smiled at them both. 'There's something really nice about that man,' Mrs March said.

When winter came the insides of Janey's thighs chafed with the cold weather, rubbing together as she walked, becoming red and raw so that it was very painful for her to move at all. At night she smeared nappy-rash cream on them which she bought herself at the chemist's and the pink lotion from the pink tube would neutralise and soothe the skin as she slept, but by the end of the next day her legs would be rubbed raw and bloody again. She walked slowly in winter and, seeing a fat girl walk slowly, people said she was lazy. But it was agony to move fast when each step meant you were skinning the inside of your thighs.

Thank God she did not have to go through that any more.

It was half past ten. The normal man still slept; well, he had been up all night, they both had. Perhaps she ought to wake him. She watched him sleeping and then laid a blanket over his body. She thought of getting under it with him, but it would be wrong. She switched off the television, having first gradually turned down the volume, so that the alteration of sound levels wouldn't be so sudden as to wake him. What a coup to have this lovely man asleep in the flat on the day after she had split with the actor. She should eat something before she went to bed, but the sight of him lying there felt so sustaining, so nutritious somehow, that anything else seemed unnecessary and anyway the normal man was smiling in his sleep.

Janey awoke early on Sunday morning. When she went into the kitchen there was the normal man making tea and cutting up triangles of bread and jam again.

'I'm really sorry, I shouldn't have fallen asleep like that.'

'Not at all. It was good to have a bit of company.'

'How are you feeling today?'

'Not too bad, my arm's a bit sore. I hope you managed to get some sleep, the floor's pretty hard in there.'

'Good for the back,' he said. He offered the plate of bread and jam to her and she took the plate from him and laid it back down on the table. He had made himself quite at home, lighting the oven and making himself a pot of tea.

'Would you mind if I gave my girlfriend a quick ring?' he asked, his hand stroking the cheek of the teapot. And he said it so calmly that Janey just thought, Oh, I see.

'Please do,' she said. The telephone was in the sitting room with the threadbare chairs. She led him there and left him to it. The difference in temperature between the kitchen and the other rooms was extreme. She went back into the warm. Soon the man joined her.

'All right?' Janey said, smiling a smile of enormous dimensions.

'Fine. I'd better be off though, or there'll be hell to pay. I hope that's OK.'

'Of course.'

'Thanks for all the jam and everything.'

'You're welc.'

He laughed and then he said, 'I don't like to leave you like this, you know, on your own.'

'Don't be silly,' she said, smiling that face-cracking smile again. 'I'm completely fine.'

'Are you sure you'll be OK?'

She nodded. Don't ask again.

'Well, I'll be in touch.' They were at the door now, and he patted the edge of her shoulder and slipped away.

Chapter 5

A MEMORY OF DAD: THE SADDEST OF ALL

It was a week before he died.

I can't write it down.

So the normal man – he wasn't a normal man at all, he was completely mad, must be – had upped and offed, without even a love you and leave you. In the kitchen on the table loomed the big red pot of jam and the large white Saturday-night sandwich loaf that the man had got for her. There was a pat of butter on a saucer, soft and yellowed at the edges, with a knife to one side. Janey picked up the knife, scooped up some butter and began smearing it over bread with a caterer's speed. She made a large plateful, eight slices cut into triangles and then cut into triangles again. Thirty-two altogether. The edges were not sharp, some looked more torn than cut, but it was not a bad effort for a one-arm bandit, she thought. She reached up into the cupboard and one by one brought down each of the pots which were kept for the men who never came to stay. There was little scarlet strawberry, sweet tip raspberry, acacia and orange flower honey, plum conserve, apricot jam for sophisticated palates and for glazing apple tarts, lemon curd and several kinds of marmalade. She could use a little bit from every jar. Thirty-two glistening, many-coloured, bejewelled pieces; they would look so beautiful and she could take a photograph of them; invite someone round for elevenses to eat them; arrange them into patterns like a mosaic or a stained-glass window. But she had not realised that cutting soft ready-sliced bread and spreading it with butter that had been in a room with the oven on was in a different league to opening new pots of jam with one hand. You just couldn't do it. Sweat trickled down her forehead with the effort. She held the first pot under the armpit of her bad arm and tried to grip it hard, digging her elbow into her side, and pulling at the lid with her good hand, but after a moment she knew that to carry on would be to force her stitches to rip open and another night in hospital, this time alone, she could do without. She gritted her teeth. She would have one last go. She took a deep breath, pressed her elbow hard into her stomach and tugged at the lid which faced downwards just below her left breast. She tried to twist its shiny rim that was slick with her hand's sweat, wrenching at it, pulling at it, but it would not give, until with a sudden yank it was off. The red jam, 'French Soft Set', oozed out of the jar and nestled into her dressing gown and nightie in great runny lumps.

She let out a low howl and began to sob and as she sobbed she picked up a lump of jam in her fingers and flattened it onto the quarters of bread, gluing several together. She opened her mouth wide and placed inside as much bread and jam as would fit. Then, working quickly, she turned round the pieces in her mouth until they became moist and she took it all down in one big swallow that hurt her throat. And the sharpness of the sugar and the tartness of the fruit reminded her how delicious food is and she repeated the process as if she were following a recipe, her right hand cupping jam which she wiped onto the bread with a stroking motion. And when the jam on her nightie was used up, and some of it had been flecked with tiny threads of Victorian white cotton, she finished off what was left in the jar with the rest of the loaf until it was all gone.

A MEMORY OF NORMAN MARCH: THE SADDEST OF ALL

Two months before he died.

We were walking round Hampstead Heath – the house in Greenly Terrace looked on to the Heath – smelling the roses and playing a game that we often played, called The Sandwich Game.

'Last night I had a sandwich for dinner and in my sandwich was lean roast beef.'

'Last night I had a sandwich and in my sandwich was lean roast beef and tomato.'

'Last night I had a sandwich and in my sandwich was lean roast beef and tomato and English mustard.'

'Last night I had a sandwich and in my sandwich there was beef—'

'Lean roast beef,' he corrected me.

'Lean roast beef, tomato, mustard and Rice Crispies.'

'Mmmmm,' Dad said.

'What on earth's wrong with that?' I asked.

'Nothing, nothing. Right then, I had a sandwich with beef, tomato, mustard, Rice Crispies and cauliflower cheese.'

'That's disgusting,' I said. 'I had a sandwich for dinner last night—'

'You did?'

'Yes, I did actually.'

'Oh actually.'

'And in my before I was so rudely interrupted sandwich I had lean roast beef, tomato, mustard, Rice Crispies, cauliflower cheese, and I also had custard powder.'

'How delightful.'

'Dad, I'm feeling sick.'

'I feel like a sandwich.'

'You don't look like one.'

He put his arm round my little waist.

Then we stopped walking. There was a small child of about four standing in front of us. He was shivering and letting out great groans of despair like an animal, completely at his wit's end.

'What's up, little one?' Dad said. 'Have you lost your Mum? Where's Mum, eh, little fella?'

The child stood stone-still. He was too distressed now even to cry.

'Don't worry,' I said. 'It'll all be fine. We'll find her for you.'

I slipped my hand into the child's hand. 'We'll just wait here until she comes back. It's all right.' I stroked his hand. 'It's all right.'

'Perhaps you would like some chocolate,' Dad said, breaking off two squares from a bar of Fruit and Nut and putting them into the child's hand. But the chocolate slipped through the child's fingers onto the ground. This made him really cry. He screamed and sobbed with all his might. 'There there,' said Dad.

'That's it, have a good cry,' I told him, 'You'll feel better for it.'

Dad started singing 'My Old Man' to try to cheer him up, doing some actions and encouraging the child to join in. And he transformed himself into a bedraggled woman running after her hapless husband, birdcage in hand, bottle in the other. The child stopped crying. He just stood without any expression at all. A few people had stopped walking to observe what had now become an act. Daddy bear, Mummy bear and Baby bear. 'When you can't find your way home,' Dad wound up the song. The word 'home' set the child off again.

About fifteen minutes had passed. The three of us sat on a bench; the child was in the middle, shivering. Dad wrapped his scarf around him; and then a woman approached.

'Johnny,' she called out and the child ran to her; the woman was crying too. She sat down with us on the bench. She thanked us for our care of her child. She was in her early twenties, she was very pale and looked ill and tired.

'Can we help you?' said my Dad.

'He ran off,' she explained. 'He's in shock. He lost his father. The weekend before last. He's taken it very badly. He keeps running off to try and find him.' She looked at my Dad.

'You look a bit like my husband,' she said. The words stopped.

'How are you coping?' Dad asked her.

She started crying. 'It's terrible. I can't bear it,' she said. 'I don't know what I'm doing. I can't go on like this.'

'It must be so hard for you,' my Dad said to this stranger.

'I can't take much more of this,' the woman said. 'How can I bear it? What can I do?'

My Dad took her hand. He took a deep breath and said something like the following:

'It's so hard just now, what you're feeling, but your life will probably never be this hard again. And you're strong and you're young and you will be able to bear it. I can see in your face how much courage you've got. And if there's one thing more powerful than fate, it's courage. And when you get through this – it'll take forever – but when you do get through it you'll be able to take on anything because you will have survived the very worst thing that can happen to a person and then the worst moment of your life will be behind you. Nothing worse can ever happen, so you have to survive this.

'And look how much he loves you,' he said, brushing the child's shoulder. At this the woman began to wail. The child followed suit and I cried too. After some minutes we all stopped crying. The woman flattened her hair with her hand and rolled up the sleeves of her jersey.

'Right,' she said. 'Into battle. Thanks. Come on, Johnny. Let's get you home, lovekin,' and the two of them walked off across the vast area of green that lay before them; there were many coloured kites flying above their heads. Dad and I remained on that bench and he cried for a minute or two, softly, with no noise that you could hear, and I held onto both of his hands.

When he had stopped crying, I said, 'It was dropping the chocolate that really seemed to make him cry. He cried like anything when he dropped the chocolate that you gave him. He really wanted that chocolate,' I remember saying.

'Perhaps something like the death of a loved one is so unbearably sad that you just can't communicate it, whereas an everyday mishap like losing something you like can be expressed by tears,' my father suggested.

'Or maybe he was feeling so unhappy that dropping the piece of chocolate was the last straw for him,' I said.

'Maybe.' We both sat thinking for a while. He circled me with his arms.

'Don't ever leave me, Janey.'

'I never ever ever will.'

Two months after that he was gone. I'd often thought about that woman since then. How strange it was that she came out with all that, at that particular time, how painful for the child to be searching for the dead man, trying to make sense of what was going on. I even went on the Heath a few times in the hope of seeing them and telling them my news after D-Day, because they would have understood. I missed that mother and that child about as much as you can miss someone you only met briefly for a few minutes one sunny afternoon.

Chapter 6

Janey sat at the kitchen table, sun pouring onto her face through the open windows, a gentle breeze giving slight motion to the blue and yellow ships on the kitchen curtains. The cathedral bells were ringing for the eleven o'clock mass. In twenty-eight hours it would be exactly ten years since he had died.

This morning, after the man had left her, her usual kitchen chair seemed uncomfortable and she couldn't keep still, rearranging the folds of her dressing gown, standing up, sitting down, moving the chair nearer and further away from the round checked table, fetching a cushion from the drawing room. There were still traces of jam between her fingers and on her night clothes and she felt sick and nauseous from the mountain of bread she had eaten – or was it disappointment and grief that were swelling her stomach and drumming at the back of her head? Where was the point in being so strict for weeks, for months on end, if you were going to blow four and a half thousand calories at one sitting? She could see an outline of the bulk inside her when she tried to pull her stomach in. She groaned as a sharp jolt of pain shot through her arm.

What was it with her and men?

It had all looked so promising. Anyone would have thought so. The way he looked at her and laughed at what she said. The hospital. *Anna Karenina. Match of the Day.*

She had forgotten to keep her expectations low, that was all. It was something you had to remind yourself to do. She remembered her first date with her actor friend when his great baby-blue eyes gazed down on her loving smile and he had taken her hand in his, kissed his lips against her lips, chinked his glass against her glass and proposed a toast to . . . to . . . she held her breath . . . to Absent Friends. Shortly after that she had dreamed that a man had asked her to marry him, going down on one knee to pop the question in some rosy bower under the arc of a hazy rainbow, and she had answered him (it made her proud to remember it), 'Don't go getting my hopes up, now.'

She propped up *Good Love? Bad Love?* on its spine and flicked through the dog-eared pages with the thumb of her good hand, separating out the leaves between her fingers when something caught her eye.

Tell the truth to yourself about what you have lost. Feel how sad it is that what you have missed no one can ever replace. Nothing can bring it back. When we were children we were helpless. We had to rely on others for what we needed. And time and time again they let us down. When we

spoke they did not hear us. When we cried they turned away.
We were told to be quiet, we were told to be good. We were
beaten. We were abused. We were blamed and we blamed
ourselves . . .

Janey put the book down. There didn't seem to be
much comfort in it after all. She got up and helped
herself to one of the chocolate buns left over from the
day before yesterday. When she had eaten it she sat
down and scraped a knife against the paper case to
release the last crumbs, which she licked from the edge
of the blade. She started on another.

It was the first year after Mr March had died.

Janey held her mother's head in her arms and
stroked her yellow hair. Her mother was still weeping.
Janey drew one of her arms away and began to stroke
the back of her mother's hand with her little finger. Mrs
March caught the finger and curled her own fingers
around it, gripping tightly. They remained like that for
some time, the elder woman seated on a chair and her
daughter standing beside her, leaning into her distress.
Janey's mother liked her to run a silver-backed hairbrush through her hair. The brush had belonged to Mr
March's mother. Although the bristles were limp and
splayed with age it had a certain severity about it, like
all her things.

'I do miss him, Mum.'

'Let's not talk about it, love.'

The hairbrush slipped out of Janey's fingers and fell to the floor.

It was a meal to remember, that first birthday after he died. Everything was done to a turn. The meat was perfectly cooked: tender, juicy, slightly pink in the middle, the way they both liked it. There was soda bread, warm and salty, to accompany the first course – 'Be careful with the ends of the aubergines,' the stallholder had said, 'they can be a bit spiteful.' Then there was mint sauce and redcurrant jelly that Janey had made to go with the lamb. The chocolate and almond cake, split and sandwiched with chestnut purée, sweetened with vanilla sugar and whipped cream, was of a lightness that the March grandmother would have been proud of. In the past, if he wasn't working, Norman March had made special birthday dinners for them and they had all eaten themselves silly, but this year Mrs March was too overwhelmed with her daughter's show of kindness to eat or say much. This Janey pretended not to notice in order that her mother's feelings might be spared, herself determined to make the most of the meal, savouring every mouthful. Having the food in your mouth made you feel so well. Those variously coloured compounds of taste, texture, aroma, those neutral compositions of molecules, those carbohydrates, globules of fat and animal and non-animal protein arranged on a plate and called food were nothing more than chance chemical make-up, substance in a way no different from insects or blades of grass or rock or metal, but the cheer they brought was immeasurable, heroic. The food was undeniably delicious. Norman March would have appreciated it, even though his favourite food, it was characteristic of him, was bread and butter, spread THICK (gravy came a close second).

Mrs March's tears cooled and salted her food as she pushed it round her plate. Janey did not know what else to do for her. The thick wedge of potato in the white ceramic dish was hot and creamy with a pale golden crust. Janey helped herself to some more.

There were thirty-five candles on the birthday cake that Janey had hidden in her bedroom. When, having turned off the lights, she brought it down all ablaze singing 'Happy Birthday To You', she felt enormously apologetic right inside her heart that all she could produce was the thin sound of one voice. Her mother believed the darkness to be hiding her tears, but the tiny beads of light given off by the flickering candles revealed the wet slippery drops on the elder woman's face and made them spangle like jewels.

'Make a wish,' Janey whispered. 'Go on, anything you like.'

That was too much for Mrs March. 'I'm sorry, darling,' she said, and ran from the room. You could hear her sobbing at the other end of the house. From the street. Janey once thought she had heard it on the

Heath. She cut a slice of cake and took it up to her mother's room, knocked gently and left it by the door. 'I've brought you some cake.' Back in the kitchen she cut herself a slice. It was very good indeed, moist, light, springy cake with the richness of the nut purée balanced by the cream. Janey cut another slice. It certainly was good cake. She sighed in its direction, looking to it for an answer. What to do with her mother. It was ten months now since D-Day. Things were not improving. Her mother needed something. I have to get her over this in one piece. If only Dad were here to help – he'd know what to do.

Janey tried to think over the question with her father's mind. It was true, Norman March had known exactly how to handle her. Caroline March, née Comrie, was highly strung, she lived on her nerves – or rather she lived on Norman's and did need a lot of handling.

Caroline Comrie met Norman March at a party. They had immediately felt for each other. He had an air of wakefulness about him which she was drawn to, but he was gentle with it and he made her laugh. He was also older, thirty-four to her twenty-three. She was shy at first, closed against him like a flower folded against the night, he had said. They talked, and as they talked her eyes, fixed on her toes (three of which peeped out of the end of her summer shoes, in descending sizes), gradually lifted to meet his eyes. His gaze for some time had focussed on her sky-blue dress, her yellow hair, her skin the colour of the palest pink roses like the ones which adorned the insides of the fine teacups they were given for their wedding. (For every cup there is a saucer.) They must have talked for nearly five hours. Caroline marvelled at all the adventures he had had; then it was her turn and, conquering her natural reserve, she seemed to unravel in great loops as she spoke, and the hand pulling the thread, his hand in hers, worked faster and faster and thoughts and feelings spun and reeled from her as they never had done before. When she told him she loved the sea, how calming and hopeful she found it, his heart was hers and before she knew what was happening, so the story went, they were driving to the Suffolk coast of his childhood holidays. There they lay on the beach. It was a cool night and Mr March fed her biscuits and whiskey from a hip flask to keep her warm, but she could not keep her teeth from chattering as they stretched out on the sand in the moonlight. To warm her, Norman lit a fire with kindling gathered from amongst the gnarled rocks that loomed over the sands on which they lay.

'You can rely on me,' he said. But what she heard was, 'You can lie on me,' and, emboldened by the drink and the urging breathy sound of the waves, she nestled up to him on that cold beach and was enwrapped in his arms. Six months later they were married. It was a sweet story that had often been told to Janey at bedtime by either parent. What she was not told then was that Caroline Comrie, born on a Monday, married on Valium. She had been taking it since she was fourteen. It was her nerves. She had to sleep between two and four every day for the same reason. Many people cry at weddings. Mrs March did and she also cried on the honeymoon. She cried almost without a break for three days and three nights. Not because she was unhappy, but because she was overwhelmed. She had never had anybody so completely for herself before and so the happiness had a searing quality to it. Mr March had understood this and he gently weaned her off the tears. At eight o'clock on the evening of the fourth day of their holiday, in their room in the discreet Dublin hotel with its white walls and dark wooden furniture, he asked her for the first time not to cry. He had arranged for two tomato omelettes to be brought up to them and there was a bottle of straw-coloured wine. And she managed not to cry for an hour as she lay in their bed with its crisp and silky Irish sheets, propped up by four frilly pillows, eating her eggs and sipping the wine that cooled her lips which were red from kissing. And he read and sang to her from a green armchair at the bedside, songs that had no heightened emotional content but were somehow relevant to their situation.

Arry Arry Arry Arry, now you've got a chance to marry
A nice little widow wiv a nice little pub
Plenty of bacca, beer and plenty of grub
I could come round and see you, and keep you company
It would be so nice for you and 'er
And wouldn't it be nice for me?

*

Caroline laughed at this because it was so far away from the truth, but she had felt a pang that she did not have such a place to welcome Norman and his friends. (Instead they were to move into his house, the house by the Heath in which he had been born, the big house in Greenly Terrace on four floors with cupboards and drawers crammed full of everything: pins, tins, ribbon, string, sealing wax, paperclips, rawlplugs, fuse wire, boxes that had contained wedding cake, lolly sticks, spare presents, eye drops, sixteen different sizes of nail. There was certainly everything anyone might need there.)

But she wasn't even a good cook. Norman sensed her spirits sinking and began another song to lighten her mood.

Oh, I must go home tonight!
I must go home tonight.
I don't care if it's snowing – blowing, I'm going
I only got married this morning.
It fills me with delight.
I'll stay out as long as you like next week,
But I must go home tonight!

She heard this song with a calmer demeanour, but his soft crooning of 'When Irish Eyes Are Smiling' in a ridiculous accent, guaranteed, he thought, to neutralise the sentiment of the lyrics, set her off again. But the next day she did leave off crying for an hour and a half in the early evening, and then for two hours the day after that and so on, until the crying almost stopped.

And they would walk the broad streets of Dublin, visiting places of historic interest, perusing glass cases full of the boots and pipes of Ireland's famous men, which between you and me, whispered Mr March, conscious of the twitchy-faced attendant, could have belonged to anyone's old Grandad. Mrs March thought it was all magical. James Joyce actually wore those boots. She imagined him pacing up and down in them, smoking a pipe, thinking up ideas, like having an embroidered picture of the Princes in the Tower hanging on the wall in the Misses Morkan's house in *The Dead* – something which had touched her immensely when her husband had read it to her in the hotel room. He loved this in her, the way she felt passionately about things which had previously left him cold.

Outside the museum, dancing up and down the curb, Norman teased his new bride by doing a mime of the great man himself, laden with collectable goods, not just boots and pipe, but extras, cape, coat, scarf, hat, waistcoat, rolled-up newspaper, matches, dirty handkerchief, a chewed pencil with traces of EXHIBIT I: JAMES JOYCE'S SPITTLE. He changed character to become an officious curator, stripping Joyce, now represented by a handy lamppost, of his treasured garments and several sundry items. Money changed hands. Norman March wrote JAMES JOYCE'S BREAKFAST EGG SHELL, A PORTRAIT OF THE ARTIST'S CANDLE-SNUFFER, on the pavement with a stone and had the curator character selling tickets for the grand finale: the unveiling of a single, detached trouser turn-up, snipped from the artist's leg when he was not looking and preserved for posterity in an alarmed glass case. Caroline, in fits of laughter, clouted him affectionately over the shoulder with her handbag. They kissed at the edge of the kerb. She sniffed back a tear, he took her hand and, laughing, they ran to St Stephen's Green where they stood beside a flowerbed filled with pink and yellow roses listening to a man crooning from the bandstand:

> If you're Irish, come into the parlour
> There's a welcome there for you.
> If your name is Timothy or Pat
> As long as you come from Ireland
> There's a welcome on the mat . . .

And a song about a woman who baked a pie with rhubarb and apple and lemon and raisins and brandy in it which could break a man's jaw. They went off to hear music in bars in the evenings and wandered about late into the night, returning to the hotel tired, laughing, half drunk and amorous.

'Shall we have seven children?' Caroline said to Norman.

'At least!' he answered her.

Mrs March had brought three nightdresses with her on her honeymoon – a white one, a pink one and a powder-blue one, each made of silk satin, calf-length, cut on the cross with shoe-string straps and sweetheart

127

neckline. To her they were fanciful, like dressing-up clothes. They had been bought in a light-hearted moment. But on the fourth night of their honeymoon when they made their first attempt at sexual intercourse it was a serious undertaking. It could not be otherwise. It did not come as a surprise to either of them that it was almost more than Caroline could bear, the love that she felt towards him and from him being so great. Before that first time she had been alarmed and hysterical at even the idea of sex, wasn't it foolhardy if you felt so close to someone in every other way to leave nothing at all for yourself? She feared that if she slept with her husband she might just dissolve into nothing. And, in fact, she did become a stranger to her notion of what and who she was when they were having sex and her brain locked into such a distant concentrated state that it frightened her. Afterwards she was caught up by so many feelings that she actually did not know where she was, or her name. And it was so hard trying not to cry in her terror that the man might fall asleep before the woman did, leaving her distraught with nothing but the soft woollen blanket that at these moments would become like sandpaper, scraping and chafing her neck and forearms. It made her feel too much, this married love. She was filled with guilt that she could not feel more at ease with it. 'I wish I could be more of a proper woman for you,' she said.

But they muddled along. Norman sang her songs and promised that he would never go to sleep before she did, a promise that he kept in their twelve years together. He encouraged her to cry and say what it was that was on her mind, built up her confidence and trust until she was strong enough not to be crippled by the enormity of her desire for him. The second week of their honeymoon was spent almost entirely in bed. She learned that sometimes there could be a lighter side to it, that their sleeping together could induce a state of mind that was akin to smiling, at a remove from anguish, from matters of life and death.

The handling of Mrs March after Norman's death fell to Janey. She was not wholly unprepared for it. She knew, for instance, that her mother needed ten hours' sleep a night, that she had to rest in the afternoons, that unless restrained she would kill plants by overwatering them. She knew that her mother did not like crowded rooms, that she needed to be on the edge of an aisle in the theatre, if she wasn't in the front row, and that alcohol went straight to her head. Sudden noises or movements appalled her. You had to make your behaviour as predictable as possible in her company. She also had to be reminded to eat or she would simply forget to do so. Janey had, in her father's lifetime, felt responsible for protecting her mother from, say, bad news in the paper or on the television, because it would completely throw her. She would cry for hours when there was a natural disaster in a foreign land, it would make her physically sick, give her a fever and a smattering of pink pin-head spots would appear on her throat and arms. Only Mr March's singing to her would lure her back to health. Or if that proved unsuccessful they would go back to the sea which had the ability to soothe her; they would float in the salty water and listen to the cries of the gulls and she would sense in the coming and going of the waves, the inhaling and exhaling of a power greater than herself. It was certainly the key to her beauty, this frailty, this brittler than eggshell sensibility. Curiously the delicateness of her person did not make her look ill. The childish, slim frame, the long and small arms, the skin which was made from such fine grain, her yellow hair, made her look like she was from another world, or even from the sea itself, a product of the calmest, sweetest waters, the softest air, an angel in a painting or a mermaid. She loved her husband because of his gentle robustness, his humour, his goodness and his lovely singing voice, and he loved her because she thought the world of him. That's how it seemed to Janey and a child's role in all this was unclear.

Now it was easy to see that Mr March had tried to raise his daughter in his own image rather than letting his wife set the example, in order that Janey's life might be more manageable than that of her mother. He had wanted his daughter to turn out resilient, fit for the ups and downs, the confusions of modern life. Mrs March's style of existence was from another era. It was an old-fashioned heroine's make-up that she had, a constitution left over from a time where the rich inhabited spa towns in the spring months. In the past she might have owned a pug for a companion, played the harp and died from a broken heart or in childbirth. She had come close to death when giving birth to Janey, they had been forced to forget the idea of seven children, but she had pulled through in the end.

How on earth will she manage without him? Janey had asked herself that day in the hospital corridor as soon as she knew he was dead. Caroline March had contained something of the young widow in her manner even when her husband was alive, the aura of a woman who was permanently recovering from some shock.

One of the first things she did after her husband had gone was to cut off her hair which had hung down in fine yellow curtains on each side of her face, so that it was short and cropped like a schoolboy's. She had to go to three hairdressers before she found one willing to commit the deed. Then there were the loose grey and black clothes she wore for years afterwards which were too severe for her colouring, lending her complexion a ghostly hue and concealing the fine lines of her figure. She went about with a face that had a scrubbed-clean look to it. It took years off her appearance, the bereavement, stripping her sense of herself as a woman and making her feel like a child, particularly a boy. She went to the sea with Janey. They caught a train to the Suffolk coast where they lit a fire and had whiskey and biscuits and just waited. Even now Janey could not smell whiskey without thinking of those terrible searches, the looking out to sea at the white sails on the horizon, the light sky, and as it grew dark the moon and the sharp stars.

*

One afternoon Janey returned home from school late. She had been helping out with junior choir practice.

> Jesus loves the Courtleigh girls
> With their dolls and with their curls
> And he loves the Courtleigh boys
> Even though they make a noise.

It had been a terrible day. One of the boys had shouted, 'Oi, Fat and Ugly Features' and she had answered, 'Yes?' which meant the whole class laughed at her until the teacher arrived and asked them what the joke was; when they said it was Janey, when they said that Janey had made them laugh, the teacher smiled at her and said, 'You are lucky, I'm terrible at telling jokes.'

She made a special supper that night. Her mother had had a lot on her plate lately and needed a bit of spoiling. There were all sorts of things that needed to be organised, his things, and it was getting her down. For pudding they had apricot and *amaretti* trifle from a *Vogue* magazine recipe.

'This is delicious,' Mrs March said. Then she started to cry. The tears dripped down her face into her dinner. Janey counted the gaps between each waterdrop. Plop: one, two, three, four, five, six, plop, one, two, three, four, plop, one, two, three, four, five, six, plop. She crossed her fingers under the table, saying under her breath, 'What can I do to make you feel better?'

'You're probably overtired. Have you slept today?'

'A bit.'

'Can you say what you're feeling?'

'Just the same; I can't bear it. I can't go on, Jane. I just can't bear it. I don't know what to do with myself, I can't seem to get through the days. What can I do?'

'You've got me, you know.'

'I know. Thank God, if I didn't have you I'd give up, I really would.'

'Well, you have got me.' Janey beamed at her mother. 'You have got me.'

'It's true I have got you,' her mother joined in. 'Thank God.'

Chapter 7

A nd so the 'normal' man had gone, and the actor, and the loaf and the pot of jam too. The allure of white food and especially the allure of white bread, with its milky appeal to lovelessness; and jam, the instant rush of sweetness, red, sharp, thick, sticky and harsh in the back of the throat. But this particular morning it was not enough to calm her. Janey cleared the table, picking up each item singly and placing it in the sink or in the yellow pedal bin. 'I put you on a pedestal, you put me in the pedal bin', she had always thought would make a good title for a song. She took a painkiller and half a sleeping pill and went to bed. She couldn't think what else to do.

When she awoke it was six o'clock on Monday morning. She had slept for eighteen hours and it sickened and shocked her to be awake. There was a dull heaviness inside her neck and chest and as she drew each breath her throat tightened so that she feared she would choke if she stopped concentrating on her breathing for a second. She sat up in bed and put her head in her good hand, tucking her chin against her chest. Very slowly she rocked herself to and fro, to and fro, to and fro. 'It's all right. It's all right,' she said.

A famous doctor, her father had told her, once treated a patient who experienced a correspondence between turning corners and going round the bend, the poor man feeling quite mad whenever the route he took caused him to veer from a straight path. Janey had often wondered if morning and mourning were similarly linked for her. When the postman had nothing for her it made things even worse. She would feel forgotten and neglected like the dead aunt must have felt in the flat for all those years, sitting on the willow-patterned chairs in the drawing room and thinking of the lovers in the willow-pattern story. The aunt who'd never married, but had stayed at home and knitted her brow, probably stung by other people's unremembering, knocked about by love maybe, the old story. Not taking any notice of someone was one of the cruellest things a person could do to another person.

The pain of loving a dead person. In less than eight hours it would be exactly ten years since her father had collapsed in the high street and died. Ten years since his heart had given out on him (he who had owned a heart that was bigger and better than anyone's). It was a combination of furry arteries from red-meat dinners every night and cooked breakfasts every morning, stress, too much drink, no exercise. All this was fine on paper but he had been so healthy, hadn't been a great drinker, had been a little overweight certainly but nothing out of the ordinary; and he'd led an active life, even the doctor said it made no sense. He didn't even smoke. And the way he ate his eggs and bacon was so nonchalant! He'd put a little bit of bacon on his fork, put his fork down, perhaps, and say a few words, then eat the bacon, then have a little toast, then wait a bit, as if thinking of something quite different, and then have a bit of egg, and a bit more egg, then pause to make some remark or other, then have a little more egg, as if he had quite forgotten the bacon, and then casually re-membering, he would go back to the bacon, wash it down with a little tea, and he'd carry on absently until he had had enough. When Janey ate, she started on her plateful and kept on at it mouthful by mouthful until it was all gone.

Why do all men love eggs and bacon so? Her father, the actor, the Scottish man. Bet the normal man liked them too. They all did.

> I like eggs and bacon, I like eggs and bacon
> But if you think I'm going to sing
> You're very much mistaken.

Ten years. It was hitting her hard, this sense of parallel time. And it was a lovely day, just as it had been then, just after the longest day of the year.

Dear Dad, Weather is fine, Wish you were here.

She counted down the minutes with the kitchen clock,

136

feeling the full force of that hour looming over her.

She fell asleep again and dreamed that he came back to her, running across the Heath in a flurry of kite tails, but in the dream she woke up alone on the grass, chilled and mocked by what she had seen. Then, still dreaming, she fell asleep on the grass and dreamed that he came alive again, and slowly he came into view, emerging from behind some bushes with two ice creams, one a plain cornet and the other a Ninety-Nine. Still in the dream, as she reached out for the ice cream with the chocolate Flake, she woke up and it wasn't true and she was alone again, even the wafery cornets had been dreamt up. After this she resolved, still in the dream, not to fall asleep any more because it was too painful; she forced her eyes to stay open, busying herself with the making of daisy-chains, terrified of sinking into dream time. Suddenly she saw him, and he was alive after all and this seemed marvellous to her, because she had dreamed twice that this would happen as if the dreams that she had dreamed had been some sort of premonition. And she was so happy to see him that she cried and cried and held him and he held her and promised that he would never leave and then she woke up and all the dreams had been the same cruel dream. He was dead as a doornail. There was no question.

Janey got out of bed and looked at her slim figure in the mirror and it struck her that she looked more unhappy than she used to. It wasn't just her face, or her eyes or round the corners of her mouth. Today there was even something a bit sad about her knees and elbows. She felt betrayed and humiliated by these joints.

Back in the kitchen, staring at the provisions that the normal man had brought her, arranged on the shelf above the sink, next to her collection of recipe books, her eyes lingered on the lettuce. It was a pale-green, densely-packed iceberg, large and shrink-wrapped. She reached up for it, batted it slightly with the flat of her good hand until it began to roll from the shelf above the sink and then she caught it in the crook of her bad arm. OUCH. She dropped it onto the table and turned away from it to get a knife and a bowl. The lettuce rolled off the table, thudded onto the floor and rolled across the blue lino through the door and into the hall. In the hall a bag of books, a pair of shoes and a jumper lay on the floor. It rolled towards the jumper and came to a halt at the neckline. Janey straightened out the sleeves of the garment and arranged the shoes so that they met its hem. She greeted the funny short person.

'All right, cabbage head?'

No reply.

'Me? Oh, I'm not so good today, actually. There was a boy here yesterday and he was ridiculously good-looking and nice as well and sort of friendly, and he read me *Anna Karenina*. Anyway, to cut a long story short he's gone off with some girl. And I broke up with this other boy on Friday as well. I think I maybe did love him quite properly, but he didn't really want me to, so I was always pretending that I didn't and then he thought that I wasn't bothered either way. And once we went to the seaside, and when I asked if I was the fattest girl on the beach, he said, 'Yes.' ('Do you want me to pretend that you're not overweight?' he added.) And I was. And this bloody arm's killing me and I don't know what the hell I'm going to write about Jane Austen. Not that you care.' She swung back her leg to take a kick at the iceberg head, but stopped at the last moment.

To love someone who's dead more than you love any living person – what a colossal waste of time! Had she got stuck, half unwittingly, arranging her behaviour in accordance with her father's wishes, drawing on a certain sort of moral energy that he subscribed to, this dead person? And watching things through his eyes, to be lovable, happy, funny and good for him (and for Her); to prepare his favourite dish (he had been buried with an enormous loaf of soda bread which Janey had made him); to sing in tune for him –

> When all your friends desert you,
> All your pals deceive you
> I'll never leave you, Bill
> Wherever you may be.
> When all the world seems on you
> They'll never take me from you
> 'Cos I know you love me, Bill
> And that's good enough for me.

– and to mend his clothes, all for nothing in return – you could not help but have misgivings about trying to please the dead in this way. You had to be both people in the relationship, running together your wishfulness with their wishfulness. And worst of all it was a way of not having any wishes of your own.

Those women in television plays who set a place for a long-gone loved one every night: knife, fork, spoon, glass, patterned napkin – that's not madness. The dead person might return, might just be found to be alive, no more bizarre than finding a living person suddenly to be dead after all. You wouldn't want a person to think you didn't care. You'd want there to be a nice hot cup of tea waiting. She gingerly kicked at the lettuce and dribbled it around the hall, pushing it and dragging it in towards her with the inside edges of her feet. But these thoughts were making her angry. 'Bloody ugly cow!' she shouted and kicked the lettuce as hard as she could straight at the skirting board; two small circles of paint fell onto the carpet. The little white chippings brought hot tears to her eyes. She made a note on the inside cover of *Good Love? Bad Love?* which was sticking out of the top of the bag of books:

> *NB. It is so unfair that being nice and generous generally makes people like you and being mean and horrible makes them hate you, because it's so enjoyable being kind and so miserable being nasty, that people ought to prefer the bad people in order to make them feel better.*

If you closed your eyes and concentrated as hard as possible you could play another game with him. You could make him come home. At the heart of her missing him was the thought that if he came back tomorrow it wouldn't be all that surprising. It would take a bit of getting used to, it would be a little disarming at first, but he'd come back to the door of the house in Greenly Terrace, through the flowerbeds, across the grass, and up to the house, calling, 'Sweet Pea, I'm home.'

'Hi Dad, good to see you.'

'Sorry love, there was a bit of a mix-up. I had to go away for a few years. Been working the halls. We took the show to Canada and New Zealand. They loved us there. I've missed you like nobody's business.'

'Missed you too.'

'Haven't you turned out lovely!'

'Thanks.'

'And Mum, is she all right?'

In time, it must have been two years or so, Mrs March had settled into something of a routine. She got up in the morning, breakfasted with her daughter and then went back to bed. She got up at lunchtime, dressed and walked round the block, sometimes twice. At 4.15 she would be standing at the bus stop to meet Janey when the school bus dropped her so that they could walk back together, calling in at a shop or two, or stopping at a café for a cup of tea. Back at home she returned to bed and got up in the evening when Janey made supper for them. Once a month she would go to the doctor's for a repeat prescription. Several brown bottles, some empty, some filled with yellow, chalky pills, lined the mantelpiece in her bedroom, over the large marble fireplace. Sometimes, on special occasions or when it had been unusually cold, Norman had risen while she lay sleeping and lit a fire in the grate for her to wake up to; then they would both lie in bed saying to each other that they were living in the lap of luxury. Once a fortnight, she would go out in the evening to a play or a film, taking Janey with her.

In bed she was industrious. She sewed, she read, she worked on a tapestry picture of flowers, sweet peas, roses and anemones in pinks and purples and reds, and she made frilled cushion covers. She darned Norman's jumpers which had grown holey through Janey's use of them. In tiny even stitches she knitted a school cardigan for Janey. The pattern said 'age 14' on it, she had ordered it over the phone along with a pair of 0.3 needles and two-ply bottle-green supersoft wool, and the department store had sent it all round. But 'age 14' was not Janey's size. She tried it on when her mother was sleeping. The buttons on the cardigan gaped four fat tear shapes when she did it up. It came down to just beneath her breasts. The sleeves just covered her elbows. Her mother mustn't find out.

'I've done something awful,' she told her mother. 'I spilt some tea on the cardigan you knitted me so I had to wash it and it's shrunk and now look at it.' She showed her the cardi, unwashed and ill-fitting. 'I'm so sorry.'

'Not to worry,' said Mrs March. 'I think the wool was very delicate. I should have told you it had to be washed by hand. You couldn't possibly have known.'

The teasing at school was getting worse. One day a wisecracker had called her 'Mammoth March' and the name 'Mammoth' had stuck. No one called her Janey any more.

'Done the Maths, Mammoth?'

'Can I see your translation, Mammoth?'

'Want to come to my house after school, Mam?'

'Can't. I've got to cook supper tonight, or she won't eat.'

Things were still very tricky for her then, in years three and four.

'What's the matter, Mum?'

'It's nothing, really. It's just that we haven't paid the gas bill and I can't stop worrying about it. If we don't pay it soon, we'll get cut off.'

'Have we run out of money?'

'No, it's nothing like that, it's just that I can't, I just don't know, I . . . ' Her mother's face creased up and her eyes closed briefly, which was always a precursor to tears.

'What is it?' Janey took her hand, her own face distorted with alarm and concern.

'I can't . . . ' her mother was speaking between the great choking sobs, 'It's really stupid, but I can't find, I . . . we . . . we don't . . . we . . . we just don't have any envelopes.'

'But Mum,' Janey was triumphant, 'you mustn't worry about that. I've got loads in my room. Pink ones from Christmas, airmail ones, plain white ones.' She left the room and returned with them a moment later.

She dropped an assortment of envelopes onto the bed. 'Look at all the envelopes we've got between us,' she said.

'Hooray,' shouted Mrs March.

'Hooray,' said Janey. They picked up envelopes in great handfuls and threw them into the air. They fluttered down onto the bed like giant confetti.

'What a wonder you are.' Her mother's voice was almost cheerful. 'What would I do without you, darling?' And the half smile she smiled and the words she spoke were like liquid gold to Janey and a sleepy, victorious contentment welled up inside her and ran into her veins.

And so the gas bill was paid and the electricity bill and all the other bills when they came round every quarter were duly paid also. Mrs March's hair grew long again and she began to look a little like her old self.

On the advice of a speaker she heard on *Woman's Hour*, Janey had arranged for a grief counsellor to visit her mother once a week at their home. 'Won't they think that too much time has gone past? Will I still qualify?' Mrs March had asked.

'I did ask about that, and they said sometimes people don't seek help for ten or even twenty years.'

'Really?'

Sydney Hiller was attached to the pastoral unit of the local council and gave his time for free. He was a kindly man, greying, with a large nose and watery eyes that looked as if they had done their fair share of crying. He had lost his mother ten years earlier under a double-decker bus. Number 19. Janey had been present at her mother's first meeting with him, where Mr Hiller told them how hard it was (the number nineteen aspect of his mother's death) because it was part of common parlance to make light of getting run over by buses. If you were late, for instance, the person who was waiting for you might say, when you finally showed up, 'At last! I thought you'd been run over by a bus!' Mightn't they? Janey and Caroline March nodded in sympathetic agreement.

Mrs Clark, who lived a few doors down, had been widowed three years back, about the same time that Caroline and Janey had lost Norman. The wife of one of the men from the music hall had died a year or two earlier. Both these people had been friends of the Marches and it wasn't long before a solemn little death club was formed for the swapping of tears, stories and handy mourner's tips. 'Feeling lonesome? Light a candle.' Janey attended the first few meetings. Each member of the group unfolded a life story and in turn received praise for the courage and good grace that had been shown. Janey was surprised at the frankness of the speakers, especially her mother's eagerness to talk, and she was impressed by Mrs Clark's talent for entertaining them all.

'On our honeymoon, it took my husband three days to become a man, dears,' Mrs Clark told the group, after Caroline had spoken of the depths of her Dublin passion. The cheerful, black-haired widow admitted after a few meetings that it was the company she came for as much as the counsel of Sydney Hiller. It was a shame that it took something bad to throw people together these days. It's ever so nice to have people to talk to, they all agreed.

'I sat down with a cup of tea the other day,' she said, 'the way you do, and I suddenly had a really strong craving. No, not that sort of craving,' she said glancing briefly down at her cleavage, which was ample (Janey often felt her eyes drawn to it; her mother was flat-chested). 'Anyway I had this terrible craving for some chocolate mousse and it just wouldn't go away. So I thought: I know, I'll go to Mr Patel's and see if he has any. So off I went and "Mr Patel," I said, "could you be so kind as to tell me if you have any mousse?" Then, to prevent any sort of a confusion I added, "Not the kind that you put in your hair, but the kind that you eat, dear." And Mr Patel goes, as straight-faced as any-thing, "No, Madam, we don't have either, nor do we have the sort with antlers on!"'

Georgie, the man from the music hall, described himself as a loner. He had lost his wife, Evelyn, several years ago. He missed her terribly even now and especially he missed her cooking which had been second to none. He thought about her every day, and when he woke up and when he went to sleep it was at its worst. Sometimes he thought about her so much that he thought it would drive him mad. It worried away at him, that she wasn't here any more, he said, like the way a dog worries sheep. But at the same time he didn't want to forget her; there'd never be anyone else.

Janey's mouth.

After a few months, extra classes after school meant that Janey could no longer attend the meetings. Her mother took the news well. There would be the three others to look out for her, after all.

That New Year, Mrs March was invited to a party. 'Will you come with me, Janey?' she asked. They made a funny little couple to look at. The thick layer of fat that Janey had grown swelled at her calves, her hips and her breasts, and gave her the appearance of someone twice her age. It made her eyes look too small for her face and her face look too small for her body. She dressed in loose clothes and long skirts that she hoped would not show the strain of having to cart all the stuff about, the fat that disfigured her, the juices that she stewed in. Only her forearms bore her natural lightness, her wrists were like a dancer's and let her know that this fat that she was coated in was not her real self. And her mother, lithe, with boyish figure and gracefulness of limb, was always at her side. They went out together, they ate together, they slept together.

So together they went off in a taxi. Mrs March, floating and wistful in a long black dress, got drunk and began to cry on the shoulder of a strange man. He put his arm around her. He was stroking her hand and giving her vodka to drink. He wiped a tear from her cheek, and folded a stray lock of hair behind her ear. Janey looked on, but her heart was in her boots. Then suddenly Mrs March's sobs became audible. Something had happened. The man had done something.

People were staring.

'It's all right,' Janey said, stepping between her mother and the man. 'I'll look after her.'

In the taxi on the way back Mrs March threw up. It was delicate, thin, clear sick. There was no food in it. Only vodka and champagne. She had forgotten to eat that day.

'Get out of my cab,' the driver said. 'Get out of the cab NOW,' he was shouting. 'You disgust me.'

'I'm sorry,' Janey said.

'Can't you keep her under control?' They got out. 'Stupid cows.' Janey started to walk off, her mother gripping onto her, and the man jumped out of the car. 'Hey, where's my fucking money?' he screamed. Janey gave him a five-pound note and didn't wait for the change. 'Slags,' he shouted after them. Her mother vomited again on Janey's suede shoes. It was about one thirty and the two women stood in the dark street near King's Cross.

'Take me home, Janey,' her mother was saying over and over again. 'I'm so cold.' She started to cry. They stumbled towards the station. Her mother's body was limp with tiredness and it was up to Janey's fat legs and arms to support them both. As they waited in a queue for a cab, Mrs March was sick again. Janey dabbed at her mother's face with a tissue, and held her hair out of her mouth. They would never get back at this rate.

When they finally entered the house, Janey released the zip on the long dress, pulled it up and over her mother's head, unhooked her mother's bra, drew her arms from the straps and guided her into bed in her white knickers. She went down to the kitchen and ate a slice of Christmas cake that she had made for them, crunching on the chalky royal icing, and then she went off to sleep in her own room. But after half an hour she relented, alarmed that her mother might feel ill in the night and find herself alone, and so she slipped into bed with her and went to sleep, her arm resting gently on her mother's slender waist.

When the man from the party telephoned the following day Janey told him firmly that Mrs March was ill and must not be disturbed.

That spring, Mrs Clark from the bereavement group fell in love with the man who had come to mend the roof after the great storm. Janey won a weekend for two at a health farm in a Spot the Difference competition (cow on the left has no yellow cowbell, milk maid on the right has only one arm, etc, etc) and presented it to them on the occasion of their marriage, the following year. Mother and child had a holiday in Ireland where Janey had her first kiss from a young sailor in Dun Laoghaire and didn't like it, although he gave her a golden anchor on a nine-carat chain and wrote her four letters from various parts of the world which she couldn't bring herself to answer. Winter came round again and Janey's legs still chafed and bled with the cold. On her fifteenth birthday she saw to her dismay that she had gained another stone.

One day, round about this time, when Janey and her

mother were Christmas shopping in Oxford Street, a double-decker bus swung out from a bus lane to overtake a stationary vehicle and hit a woman who was crossing the road carrying several bags bearing the racing-green chevron logo of the John Lewis chain. She was not seriously injured, the driver had pulled on the brakes just in time to spare her from all but a little knock, but still, a little knock from a double-decker bus is serious and Mrs March was an eyewitness. Without pausing for thought she hauled a man out of a phone box so that she could ring for an ambulance and then she ran to the aid of the woman, helping her carefully to the pavement, taking the strain of her weight on her shoulder and forearm. Janey followed them with the woman's carrier bags that were trailing red tinsel and splinters of metallic Christmas balls which crunched underfoot. The woman went off in an ambulance, lying on a stretcher surrounded by carrier bags, having thanked them all over and over again. That evening Mrs March wanted to sit up talking late into the night.

'When we were first married everyone used to come to Norman with their problems, somehow thinking that he'd have the answer. The phone never stopped ringing with people wanting to know things, where there was an all-night chemist, how late they should let their children stay up on school nights. People wrote to him from miles away asking what he would do in their shoes, over love affairs or money, anything at all really, where to get a good pair of walking boots. Anyway, I felt a bit like him today. It had never occurred to me how good it must have made him feel.'

'I'm sure it did. I'm going to make a hot drink. Would you like one, Mum?'

'No, I'll make them, you go up and keep the bed warm. I'll be up in a moment.'

The following morning, when the alarm clock heralded the chill winter dawn, Mrs March sprang out of bed and said to her daughter, 'Rise and shine, lazybones, seize the day!'

As Janey was working hard for her exams it was decided that Caroline would take over the cooking for a while. Her style of cooking was different from her daughter's. They had both chiefly learned their kitchen skills from Mr March, but Janey's fondness for recipe books had led her further afield from the traditional British fare that her father had favoured. When Mrs March cooked, the two of them ate as he had done. Hearty soups, raised pies, steak and kidney, beef in beer, apple crumble, fish cakes and parsley sauce.

It was funny being cooked for, it was difficult to eat when you didn't know exactly what had gone into the food that lay before you, when you didn't know what time it would be ready or if there was more to come. You didn't know how to pace yourself with your plateful if you weren't told if pudding had been made or whether there would be nothing else when you had finished what was on your plate, except perhaps an apple. And her mother would sometimes do things wrong. She would cook the vegetables for too long, leave the odd lump in custard or mash when it would have been better out, she would forget to make the crumble topping with brown sugar and oats and nuts. The food stuck in Janey's throat and made her heart sore. She found herself eating less and less at meal times. Her mother put this down to the stress of exams.

The Happy Chip was a fish and chip shop that Janey passed on her way home from school every day. Most days she would saunter up there before she took the bus home to Greenly Terrace, stuffing her blazer and her hat into her school bag as it was a rule that Courtleigh girls were not allowed to be seen eating in their uniform (Courtleigh girls are courteous girls) and local shops had been asked to report any pupils who were caught doing so.

There was a fruit machine in The Happy Chip adjacent to the eye-level heated cabinet filled with battered saveloys, reddened chicken quarters, plastic-wrapped pies and knobbly fish portions. So she would get a bag of chips and smother them in salt and vinegar, vinegar so dilute that you could only taste it if you put on enough to make it seep through the paper and drip out the other side. She'd eat these chips whilst playing on the machine, mesmerised by the red and gold lights that swept up and down the tilted front of the unit, gently lulled by the tinny, repetitive jingle. The buttons on the machine became shiny and slick from the vinegar and grease and sometimes when she reached the fast nudge or the 'Crock of Gold' feature, and the jingle became faster and louder with her heartbeat and the pattern of lights danced and dizzied her eyes, her hands would slip and the reel of fruits would move down two symbols when she had only intended one, and a high cash payout would escape through her fingers. Boys from Courtleigh Boys school used the shop as well, crowding the one red plastic table and four plastic chairs that stood between the counter and the door, and Janey would generally leave as they arrived, anxious that their fierce taunting of each other might extend to her. If she hadn't lost all her money by the time she had eaten the chips, she'd buy another bag for the way home. She did not much like the taste of chips. There was the smell of ashtray in the stale fat they were cooked in, the vinegar made them soggy and they were overcooked so that what should have been fluffiness on the inside was woody and had a texture of collapse to it, like an overripe Cox's. Eating in a hurry, so as to be finished before the boys arrived, the edges of the crisper chips felt hard and sharp as if they might cut into her insides as she swallowed them. The damper pieces felt as if they might roll into a choking ball of potato that would stick in her throat. But the heat and the salt and the feeling of something warm in her hands and in her mouth was just right.

To tempt Janey, who remained off her food, Mrs March would ask her every morning what she would like that night: 'Steak, ice cream, fish pie, Parma ham sandwiches? Can you give me an idea of what you might like?'

'Anything's fine.'

'You say that, darling, but whatever I make doesn't seem to be right.'

'It's not the food, it's just that I get so tired after I've been at school all day.'

'But you must eat or you'll get ill. Perhaps you're sickening for something. I'm going to the doctor in the morning; why don't you come along?'

'I don't need to see a doctor.'

Mrs March, you've brought your daughter here because she's off her food. Frankly I find that difficult to believe. Look at the size of her. Are you aware that she has been patronising an establishment called The Happy Chip and regularly consuming up to one pound twenty's worth of chips? Didn't you smell a rat when you saw the vinegar stains on her socks?

'I know, why don't you make a list and I'll get whatever you like.'

'But I'll cook it though?'

'Of course you could, darling, I just thought it would be easier for you if I did, what with you having so much homework these days and my being at rather a loose end.'

'But I like to do the cooking. I find it relaxing. It's sort of like a hobby.'

'But do you think it's a good idea though? I mean, you're so tired when you get back from school and you always prepare everything so beautifully.'

'Honestly, I don't mind in the least.'

'I know you don't but I just feel it would be better if I did it.'

'Just let me do it, just this one thing, just let me do it, all right?' Janey screamed at her mother for the first time in her life and immediately flushed with shame; it was like striking out at a baby. Calmly, she added, 'I've never asked you anything, just let me do this. Please.'

Janey went back to cooking the supper for the two of them and it was never discussed again. It was a relief to both of them to go back to normal. Janey's appetite came back. She still called in at The Happy Chip on her way home as it felt like a rather festive way to celebrate the end of the day and to steel herself for the many hours of revision that lay ahead; also, it had become something of a habit.

In the fifth year after D-Day the little bereavement group started to meet twice a week. Over the years it had taken on a new academic aspect. Now they read articles on grief and larger issues of mental health; each member would speak on a topic for the benefit of the others, handing out diagrams, data and photocopied essays to illustrate the points they made. They discussed the medication they took and investigated side effects. George's heart pills, they discovered, were being prescribed with something of a cavalier attitude and a second opinion from a different doctor pronounced them wholly unnecessary. Mrs Clark admitted that she had become dependent on slimming pills but had weaned herself off them because of the violent mood swings they produced. They still reminisced, reworked deathbed scenes and the grieving process, anger, denial, role play, disillusionment, acceptance, and so on, and they still exchanged jokes, but the group had certainly moved onto a more analytical footing. One evening Caroline March had admitted to the group, in Janey's presence, that she had been taking tranquillisers since she was fourteen, but that in the last year she had gradually managed to reduce her dosage, with the doctor's help, to next to nothing. Mrs Clark began to clap, Sydney Hiller joined in and Georgie started singing 'For she's a jolly good fellow'. Slightly stunned by this news, Janey made her mother a cake in the shape of a basket of roses to celebrate.

Mrs March was beginning to toughen up a little. It seemed to her after this time-lapse that the inclination of others to treat her like an invalid all her life had given her some preparation for her widowhood. With the help of Sydney Hiller, Mrs March had identified a foreboding that had afflicted her mother and father, her husband, in fact anyone she had come into contact with; there was some idea that unless they were all constantly vigilant, something awful would happen to her. Her parents had taken her everywhere with them, never let her out of their sight, insisting on quietness for her and special treatment, the featheriest, fluffiest pillows and the whitest covers for their little princess at sleep. It seemed to her now that she had spent almost her entire childhood in bed, listening to the other children playing out in the street beneath her bedroom window, staring at the leaf pattern on the heavy curtains that tried to persuade her it was nighttime when there was broad daylight on the other side of the glass. And as she lay there in her little white cast-iron bed she had longed for the day when she would be well enough to live a bit more.

Caroline March's mother had been forty-one when she had given birth to her prematurely and there had been complications, but the baby had made a complete recovery apparently, there had been no real cause for their continued alarm. Only, the vast changes in her mother's circumstances – love, marriage, a family, all coming at a time when she had given up hoping for them – made everything so precious that the idea of losing any of it, though unthinkable, was never far from her mind. Her father felt so much for the tiny child that even to look at her or touch her made him terrified of harming her in some way. Caroline had taken this on board, reading these signs of caution as the signs of love.

But five years after her husband had died it dawned on her, amid the small formal gathering of people, that the consideration, the kid gloves and the cossetting she had been shown by her parents, by Norman, even by little Janey, did not correspond to any fixed insufficiency within herself. In fact their extreme form of care had allowed her to bank her resources, and her mechanisms for coping, as-tonishingly, did not reveal themselves as decayed or rusted beyond repair, but were actually stronger and more resilient through being unused. And she did feel strong now. She could shoulder any manner of mishap flung at her.

Their bed became a measure of this change of heart. At fifteen Janey had attempted to wean her mother off the presence of her body in bed at night. And they had struck an agreement that they would only sleep together on Mondays, Wednesdays and Fridays, with a view to Mondays and Fridays only after six months. But Mrs March had made it impossible for them to stick to this. Often there had been tears at bedtime and Janey simply did not have the heart to say No to her mother; they had none of them ever had the heart to say No to her. So it came as something of a surprise to Janey when on her sixteenth birthday her mother announced that the present sleeping arrangements would have to stop and they must both keep to their own beds in future.

Mrs March, through some curious gift of God, had taken on a new lease of life. She signed up for day and evening classes. World religions, Tango, Women's Growth, Stretch and Tone. She seemed to be rediscovering her youth. Out together, mother and child were frequently taken for sisters. 'I'm having my delayed adolescence,' Mrs March said. She'd even started to get the occasional outbreak of spots on her face.

One day, whilst out buying vegetables for the weekend in the market together, Caroline and Janey had visited a fortune-teller at the back of his crystal showroom off the Camden Road. He had made them both stand in front of a mirror and chant 'I forgive everybody everything' one hundred times each and then, 'I love and respect myself.'

'This is stupid,' Janey said.

Tarot Tim answered in his cool, smoker's drawl, 'Just say it, let go, act as if you believe it.'

'Come on, Jane,' said Mrs March.

'I tell you what, I'll wait outside,' said Janey.

Through the iridescent beaded curtain she saw the fortune-teller write out a prescription for Mrs March which she read back to him: 'I love and respect myself. I forgive everybody everything. I am a whole, perfect, beautiful human being. Today I will be happy. I will not say No when I mean Yes. I will speak the truth at all times and if I make a mistake I will admit it readily. I will not criticise others, they may be wrong but I will not say so. Today I will be grateful that I live in this beautiful world of opportunity, and as I give to the world, as I give to the great and lovely world, so the world will give to me.'

'Ideally, you want to read this out loud when you're in the nude,' Janey heard the man say. 'Perhaps you could get your daughter to say it too. Something's blocking her. She's carrying too much weight around, it's not healthy. She needs to know that she's a woman. Does she have a boyfriend?'

'Cheek!' thought Janey.

From then on, Caroline March started each day with a series of affirmations that were spoken naked into a full-length mirror. The words rang out of the bedroom into the hall and up to Janey's own room and she shut the door. Why they assaulted her in a way the tears had not done, she did not know.

Janey's role in the household became a little uncertain. There were no obvious areas that remained hers. Her mother had acquired a new vocabulary that inhibited their behaviour. If Janey talked about a recipe or the cheapness of the raspberries in the market, her mother would look at her with suspicious eyes which said, 'You speak of food, but what is it you are really saying?' And when she in turn hinted at the new strength she was acquiring, the words repelled her daughter. Why couldn't they have carried on as before? Singing and talking about people and things and laughing in the big house together until they were old ladies.

> Dear old Pals, jolly old Pals
> Clinging together through all sorts of weather
> Dear old Pals, jolly old Pals
> Give me the friendship of . . .

Jancy still continued in the way that was familiar to her. She arranged certain matters, sent off cheques, paid the bill at the Italian food shop where they had an account, bought light bulbs and boxes of tissues by the dozen, only to find that these tasks had already been done. Janey still shielded her mother from bad things; for example, she did not see fit to mention the horse that was injured by a bomb in Hyde Park, nor did she tell her about the fire at King's Cross station that claimed so many lives (and King's Cross only a few miles a way), only to overhear her mother relating these things to Mrs Clark, over a cup of tea, with no visible distress. Her mother had started hiding things from her, or at least she no longer told her daughter everything. Janey half longed for the dark evenings of the past, when a trembling Caroline would unfold her catalogue of troubles and, sick with worry at the seriousness of her mother's distress, Janey would do her best to attend to it. This daily round, strange treasure that it was, had ended abruptly. Fool's gold it seemed to Janey now.

Now when Janey looked at the pie chart with its four segments labelled OK (baby pink), Overweight (slightly brighter pink), Fat (shocking pink), Obese (deep rose colour), she found that her weight and height measurements just qualified her for the darkest section.

Most of all she longed for her mother's bed.

Going out on a spring day with a thick jersey and a scarf and gloves, Mrs March said, just as Janey took a step towards getting their coats, 'That was the annoying thing about Norman, he always made me wear a coat when we went anywhere, unless there was a heat wave on.'

'It is quite cold out, you know.'

'For goodness sake, Janey, stop fussing.'

'I thought we might go out for dinner this year,' said Mrs March when her birthday came round again.

'Oh, I was going to cook something.'

'That's very kind of you, but I thought it would be good to get out for a change.'

So they went out. Mrs Clark and her new husband Reggie, Georgie, Sydney Hiller, Janey and a couple of her mother's new friends – a newly divorced female psychotherapist who was prone to bouts of hysterical weeping, and the skinny woman who ran Mrs March's exercise class.

Janey hated eating out apart from at The Happy Chip where she was still something of a regular. The meal was a strain. She felt suspicious of the food that was served, which seemed pretentious somehow and vastly over-priced. She sat edgily, waiting for it to be over, unsure of herself and her surroundings, anxious about some possible outcome, and, in fact, something awful did happen. As Janey pushed the three little char-grilled scallops round her plate, under and over their bed of dandelion leaves, the psychotherapist, Saskia, attempted to engage her in conversation.

'Not hungry?' she asked, head inclined, mouth locked into a smile of broad understanding.

'No, not really.'

'I see,' the woman nodded knowingly.

'What d'you see?'

'Well, it must be hard for you. I imagine in the past, on such occasions, it's just been you and Mummy, eh? I see it might be difficult having to share her suddenly, to metabolise the change in your relationship.'

'What d'you mean?'

'Nothing.' She increased the angle at which her head was inclined. 'Only Caroline's told me how difficult things have been for you, letting go of the special closeness that a child and a parent, especially a child and a mother, share. I just wanted to congratulate you really and to say keep up the good work.'

Janey sat quite still for a moment, then she removed the cutlery from her plate and gently and privately tipped its contents into the other woman's lap.

'Stupid old crow,' Janey hissed and got up and left. The plate slipped onto the floor and broke loudly.

(Mr March had positively looked forward to the rare occasions when visitors had accidentally knocked things over and broken them at the house in Greenly Terrace because he so enjoyed reassuring the offender. 'Please don't give it another thought,' he'd say. 'You know, quite honestly we're glad to see the back of it. Between ourselves, you've actually done us rather a favour.')

Making her way home through dimly lit, rainy streets, shaking and fuming, Janey weighed the woman's words. They were not the opposite of the truth.

They had all treated Mrs March like a rare and beautiful cracked cup, terrified of giving her anything to hold in case the crack should open and the life force should spill out. But as the dosage fell away to nothing and Mrs March began to enter into life in a way that she had never done before, the crack hadn't opened at all, only some quantity of poison had leaked out of it and now the crack was invisibly mending itself.

Unspeakably and by tiny degrees, it began to dawn on Janey that they had none of them been doing her mother any favours by feeding her and undressing her, by keeping anything that wasn't lovely from her. And through some great mistake in understanding, as they had tended to her, it was the incapacity that had flourished, the illness that had grown lively and strong. This thought churned and seethed inside Janey, accusing and humiliating her in turn. She cried into her chips, and into her pillow at night. What they had done had been criminal.

Chapter 8

Monday 23rd June. Eleven o'clock. He had died at 3 p.m. There had been nothing in the first post. When the second post came there were three envelopes. The first was from Janey's mother.

> *Just a few words to say that I am thinking of you today and that I know that if Norman were alive he would be so proud of his beautiful, clever daughter. Please don't cut me out.*
>
> *Best love, Mum*
> *X*
> *PS. Love you.*
> *PPS. I'll call round later on, if you don't want me to, phone.*

On the front of the card there were some lilies.

The second card was from Edward. It said so on the back of the envelope, where it also said BY HAND. She didn't know anyone of that name. There was a small tissue-paper package enclosed. It was the ring that the nurse in the hospital had left in the normal man's safe-keeping. HIM. There was a slip of paper with it, on which was written:

> *Dear Janey March, like the month,*
> *I'm so sorry about what happened on Friday night. I hope you are OK. Please ring if you want to, or I'll ring you.*

Then his phone number and then:

> *I meant to give this back to you yesterday, but I forgot to.*
> *See you soon, I hope,*
> *Edward*

The last envelope had a supermarket logo on the front of it. Janey was always sending off for vouchers and special offers. Inside there was a letter.

Dear Janey

************ CONGRATULATIONS **************

The Price Cuts promotional department has great pleasure in informing you that your slogan for our new chain of baked potato outlets:

AT SPUDDIES WE CATER FOR EVERY TASTE IN POTATA

has been judged by our panel to be the winner in our competition.

* * * * * * * * * * * * * * * *

Your prize is a three-minute supermarket trolley-dash at the Price Cuts store of your choice, on a date to be arranged at your convenience in July. At Price Cuts you'll be able to put your hands on everything you need – all those snacks, biscuits, delicious chocolates, scrumptious desserts, drinks and cakes the kids love. And don't forget all those soups, cans of tuna and salmon, vegetables and fruit, too. At Price Cuts we have all the basic essentials, coffee, tea, breakfast cereals . . . And don't forget those household items such as cooking foil, washing powder, cleaning products and toilet paper.

Please telephone Mrs Hewitt at Promotions to make the arrangements.

In addition to this we will be using your slogan in our nationwide advertising campaign, so you will see your slogan in the press. We target women's magazines and teenage publications. You will also be able to hear it on local radio stations. There will be a poster campaign in the major cities and we are looking into television possibilities.

We look forward to meeting you and awarding you with your prize and the Miss Spud crown before long.

Congratulations once again,
Happy Shopping Now!

Steve Crinkle
Marketing Manager

Janey sat down. She didn't know whether to laugh or cry. She put the kettle on. She felt cheered by the prize. What a mad few days it had turned out to be.

She should eat some healthy food. A bowl of cereal with an apple grated on it. Not to be terrified and obsessive about food, all you had to do was know that you were allowed to have three meals a day of whatever you wanted, stop eating when you were no longer hungry, and not eat in between. Then your body would find a shape that was comfortable and healthy for itself. She put the cereal in a bowl. There weren't any apples.

She had lost the weight the wrong way, lived on her nerves and half starved herself; but she could try to keep it off the right way. It wasn't an admission of failure every time you put food in your mouth. It was easy to over-eat or to eat nothing, but eating sensibly was what was so hard. She poured some milk on the cereal and tried to eat it slowly. It was not unknown for her to eat her dinner in the commercial break of a soap opera.

Being crowned Potato Queen was a bit rich. Perhaps she could refuse the Miss Spud title. It was a bit too close to the bone, somehow. And what about the boys? Which one should she call? Both? Neither? The actor: better the devil you know; out of the frying pan . . . ? Or the normal man: pastures new and all that? Whatever. It really didn't matter. Would she go for all meat in the trolley-dash or sensible household goods? You weren't allowed cigarettes or alcohol. Not having a fridge was going to be a problem, perhaps she ought to buy one. She could get a year's supply of loo paper – boring – all the jam she could cram into the trolley – fatttening, and a lonely reminder that no men ever came for it, and heavy to carry home alone. How on earth would she get all the stuff home? Surely they would provide transport. And what if her arm hadn't healed by then? She would be rushing round with an arm in a sling, knocking it against God knows what, only able to grab one item at a time. It was so unfair. Perhaps they would allow her extra time if she turned up injured, or she might be allowed to have a helper. How romantic! And then she'd never manage it all on the bus, all that stuff, mineral water by the bottleful, sweets, crisps, tins of tomato soup falling down on top of her; things that would keep or luxury goods with limited shelf-life; jars and jars of coffee, but she didn't drink it; bars and bars of chocolate, but she wasn't meant to eat it; frozen chips, purple shimmering foil wrappers coming towards her; boxes of cakes, hundreds and thousands raining down on her; smoked fish swimming at her in great orangey pink packets; ground almonds; olive-oil bottles clanking; poultry; pulses; proteins . . . the products whizzed round her head in all their packaging, dizzying, blinding her until all that was left was a big white blank. And then a picture of her father. 'Quieten down now,' he was saying. 'It's all right, Sweet Pea. All right.'

This whole prize thing wasn't going to help with her food obsession, or at least it was helping it along like nobody's business. Alarm bells were ringing.

Dr Snellford at the clinic, tall, dark and devilishly handsome: 'You think about food all the time because it is less painful to think about food than to think about how much you miss your father.'

Maybe. She'd been seeing him for a month now, at her mother's insistence and expense. (Her mother had embarked on a course which after seven years would entitle her to practise as a psychoanalyst.) Dr Snellford said the reason she was so unhappy about her father's death now, particularly, was because she had been pushing down all her feelings with food for so long, and since she had stopped eating they were all popping up again and she had to face them without the drug she had come to rely on.

'Sort of cold turkey?' she said, and laughed. Dr Snellford kept a straight face.

'But,' said Dr Snellford, 'thinking about food and weight and NOT eating all the time has become a new way of bingeing, mental bingeing, without having to take in the food, and this serves the same kind of function as compulsive over-eating. It is a different drug, but a drug nonetheless.'

It all sounded fairly likely, up to a point, maybe. It was certainly the kind of thing that people said. Her father sometimes said to people with whom he partially disagreed, 'I know that is a point of view.'

'I know that is a point of view,' said Janey. She looked up at the psycho doctor for some sort of sign, a raised eyebrow, a wan smile, a look of compassion, boredom, a psycho-handshake, a wink, a kiss?

'Talking like this makes me feel hungry,' said Janey.

'Good,' said the doctor. 'That means we're getting somewhere.'

Miss Spud though, well, it wasn't exactly dignified. She'd have to paint her face waxy yellow and roll in some mud. Great. It wasn't quite the image she was aiming for in life.

It was going to be embarrassing to have to explain it to the psycho. He might advise her not to accept the trolley-dash. But there was no cash alternative on offer. She could always do something really mad like give it all to the local children's ward. It was a rather choice dilemma anyway, out of the ordinary, lacking in the workaday aspect that usually gave worrying a dreary quality. If they would let her wait until her arm healed, she would do well. She was good with a trolley; to some people they were unwieldy, but Janey had often noticed that she seemed to have more skill than the next person when it came to manoeuvring them.

On the kitchen table, with its blue and white formica top, she laid some sheets of paper and began writing: 'Who do I want to see today?' She made three columns and drew a line across the page an inch from the top to make boxes for three headings. She wrote the words: 'Mum', 'The Actor', and 'The Normal Man'. Next to each name she wrote the appropriate telephone number. Next to each phone number she drew a receiver, an old-fashioned round dialling model for her mother, a slightly outmoded long and narrow trimphone in two tones of blue for the actor and one of those white phones with a squarish base and black buttons (probably called a Viscount or a Tribune) for the normal man. She didn't really care. Sometimes, if you were going to be with someone, it might just as well be one person as another. The fact that someone is a person is frequently their most striking characteristic.

The difference between being alone and being with someone is much greater than any superficial distinctions of personality. In fact she rather felt like being alone. She laughed. Sometimes it only takes one to tango. Two can be a crowd. Just then the telephone started ringing and she let it ring for twelve rings before she answered it.

'Hello?'

'Hello.'

'I'm just ringing to see how you are.'

'I'm fine, actually.'

'Good.'

'How are you?'

'I'm good.'

'Good. Um . . . Who is this, please?'

'It's Edward, you know, from the other night.'

'Oh, yeah. Thanks for sending the ring.'

'You got it all right then.'

'Yes, it's right here in front of me.'

'On your finger.'

'No, on the kitchen table.'

'Near the jam.'

'Well the jam's in the cupboard which is fairly near the table, you might say.'

'It was good jam.'

'Good.'

'So, what you up to?' he asked.

'Oh, this and that.'

'Two jobs, eh?'

'Very funny.'

'But seriously, are you busy?'

'What, right now?'

'Right now.'

'No. Not really. Why?'

'I was wondering if I could come over and, you know, colour in your afternoon.'

'Could do.'

'Would you like me to?'

'I would, quite.'

'Shall I see you in about an hour then?'

'OK, if you must.'

'I must.'

'See you then, then.'

'See you then then, then.'

'See you then.'

'Bye, then.'

'Bye.'

'Goodbye.'

'I hope you're not about to call me Squidgey.'

'Nothing could be further from my mind.'

'I'm putting the phone down now.'

'So am I.'

'One two three.'

'Bye.'

'Bye.'

'I warn you, I'm in a bit of a state and the house is in a mess and I'm covered in spots.'

'Cool.'

'Bye then.'

'Janey?'

174

'That's my name, yes.'

'I went to a café this morning.'

'Don't you work?'

'I've got a week off.'

'For good behaviour?'

'Something like that. Anyway, I had a cappuccino.'

'So?'

'Well when it arrived, you know the way they sprinkle chocolate on the top?'

'I do, yes.'

'Well the chocolate had somehow arranged itself in a heart shape.'

'Fancy that.'

'Just thought I'd let you know.'

'You'll be talking about sunsets and rainbows next.'

She paused.

'How's your girlfriend, anyway?'

'She's all right. A bit hysterical. She gave me the elbow, actually.'

'Does that seem . . .' she searched for a neutral word . . . 'very annoying?'

'I'll live.'

'Yeah?'

'It's fine. And . . . oh yeah, how's your arm?'

'It's on the mend.'

'Good.'

Neither of them spoke for a few seconds. Then Janey said, 'Anyway we won't have anything to say if we talk too much now.'

'True.'

'Let's say goodbye.'

'OK.'

'Bye.'

'Bye.'

Janey replaced the receiver with a clank.

The normal man arrived with a shocking-pink geranium in a green plastic pot. Janey showed him into the kitchen and put the flower on the table.

Mr March, in his own words, had had a green finger for geraniums and the garden of their house in Greenly Terrace had been full of them. He had gone out there most mornings, making his way down the stony path that divided the beds and lawn in two, to rehearse his jokes with a bit of privacy. 'I do like to try out a new joke on the geraniums,' he used to say. Janey and Caroline sometimes tiptoed behind him and he would pretend not to see them, not to hear their stifled giggles at his funny stories. Then suddenly he would swing round and catch them. At first he would pretend to be furious and they would race back down the garden path into the house, but his feigned anger would soon evaporate because, he maintained, both girls were about as near to being flowers as was humanly possible. To prove it, he'd call Janey Sweet Pea and Caroline he would call Petal.

Sometimes when they went to the cemetery they would take some of his geraniums to leave on the grave, in pots so that they would stay alive. Janey placed them where she felt his belly to be, as she had often buried her face in the soft wool of his jersey there, as a little child, when anything had troubled her. Once, soon after he had died, she lay down on the grave itself for a few minutes, trying to circle the mound of new grass with her arms. They seldom went into the garden after he had gone. A man came for three hours a week to tend to it so that it would not go into a decline, but it was Norman's place and without him, without his flowers, it wasn't the same.

The normal man stood by and watched Janey's face crumple and tears begin to fall.

'What's the matter? Is it your arm?'

'No, no, it's just that my father used to grow geraniums before he died and . . . '

'And it makes you think of him.'

'Yes.'

'And you still miss him a lot?'

'Yes, I do.'

'Poor you, it must be awful. And your poor old arm as well.'

'I know.'

'Such a nice arm, too.'

They were silent for a moment. Then the man said, 'I think I know how you feel because when my mother died, the smallest things would set me off. If someone said the word 'mother' even. She was really mad about custard cream biscuits; most days she would have two at teatime – she really looked forward to them – even now when I smell them it affects me, so I know exactly what you mean about the flower. You can't help associating people with the things that they liked, the things that made up their lives.'

'I know.'

'Do you ever cry?' she asked him.

'What, emotionally or onionly?'

She laughed. 'You know, for your mother.'

'Yes I do.' Again they were quiet for a few moments until the man said, 'How long ago was it that your father died?'

'Ten years ago, in fact ten years ago today.'

'No wonder you're feeling the pinch then.'

'How long for you?'

'Fourteen years.'

'Unless it was last week people think you've got over it, don't they?'

'I know.'

'How old were you when it happened?'

'Eleven.'

'Me too . . . Edward?'

'Yeah?'

They were seated opposite each other at the kitchen table. Janey got up for a moment and reached down the custard creams that the normal man had bought for her from the shops the day before yesterday. She put them next to the potted geranium. They sat with these two items between them.

'It's a little altar to our dead,' Janey said. 'Do you mind if I hold your hand?'

The normal man reached out for her hand and she

closed her eyes and they both sat like that for some time, drinking in the fellow feeling, joined at the finger tips.

A sharp ring on the doorbell broke the spell. It was the actor. He had brought her a bunch of cornflowers. He had never given her flowers before.

'What have you done to your arm?' he said.

'It's a long story. Come in.'

Janey led him into the kitchen and drew another chair up to the table. She introduced the two men. They looked quite alike. Perhaps there wasn't much to choose between them. People were very similar, often. The three sat together in silence.

'What's new, Jane?' the actor said.

Nothing was new, everything was old. Janey herself felt old. Older than the lace tablecloths in the linen cupboard that were too fragile to be unfolded, older than the unkissed bones of her dead great maiden aunt, older than the hills, older even than the 'old story'. She looked round the room for something to hold onto. She read the lettering on her dead aunt's storage jars: TEA, BEANS, COFFEE, SUGAR, RICE, RAISINS, FLOUR, OATS. Then she started to laugh.

'I knew there was something,' she said. 'I've won a supermarket trolley-dash – in a competition.'

'You've done what?'

'There was a competition in a magazine and I won it. It's at Price Cuts.'

'Congratulations,' said the normal man.

'Good for you, Jane,' said the actor.

Dead said the doctor, dead said the nurse,
Dead said the lady with the alligator purse.

They discussed which items she would go for.

'What did happen to your arm?' the actor asked again. 'I mean, I leave you alone for five minutes . . . '

'She had an accident.' The two men were looking at each other.

'Oh, right,' the actor said. 'Well.' He got up. 'I think I'll leave you to it.'

Janey showed him to the door. 'Thanks for the flowers,' she said.

'You're welc.' And then, shyly, 'Could I see you sometime? Perhaps we could have a dance one of these nights?'

'Yeah, I haven't really got my dancing legs on at the moment, but maybe in a week or two.'

'Whatever . . . Janey?'

'Yeah?'

'Love you.'

'Love you too.'

They both stood by the door, looking down.

'Will you ring me tomorrow?' she asked him and he nodded and very gently kissed the swollen little finger of her bad hand. She opened the door for him. There stood her mother, dressed in a blue flowery summer dress, face startled, her thumb half an inch from the bell.

'Having a party?' she said. She took in the foam-rubber sling. 'What have you done to your arm, darling?'

'I cut it on some glass, by mistake.'

'Are you sure?'

'A man knocked into me at a party and his glass broke against my arm.'

'Was he drunk?'

She hadn't even thought of that.

'How are you feeling in yourself, though?' her mother was asking now.

'Rough,' Janey replied.

She took her mother into the kitchen and introduced her to the normal man. He got up to go but sat down again on catching Janey's eye.

'The flat's looking really nice, love. Juliet always did have such good taste.'

'I know, poor old thing,' said Janey.

'What makes you say that?'

'Well, you know . . . '

'No, I don't. What do you mean?'

'You know, living here all on her own. I'm sure she minded not having anyone to look after or anyone to look after her. All that endless washing and everything.'

'What gave you that impression?'

'It's just what her life was like, you can tell. There's something sad about this place, and sort of brave, falsely cheerful. Mr Lord said that her life had been a constant strain . . . '

'On him, maybe,' Mrs March laughed. 'You've got the wrong end of the stick somehow. Juliet was one of the brightest women I've ever met. Men went mad over her well into her seventies, she had them for breakfast! She must have had at least three proposals of marriage by the time she was eighteen. After that, I don't know, perhaps four a year on average until she was really quite old. But she had vowed at the age of ten never to marry, couldn't see the point somehow, and she kept to her word. Honestly, there were endless love affairs. We never knew how she had the energy. Ambassadors, wealthy businessmen, soldiers. She always had a soft spot for army men. She could wind them round her little finger! People said she'd grow out of it, but she never seemed to. She was an amazing woman. One of the great beauties of her day. How do you think she got this flat? The family didn't want much to do with her, though, you can imagine, but I've always thought she was rather a star.'

'I just can't believe it,' said Janey.

'I wonder why?' her mother mused.

'I mean, why did she let the flat get into such a state?'

'Well, for one thing she was hardly ever here. She was always going to stay with people. But the master bedroom's in good order isn't it? She'd have made sure of that.'

'Yes it is,' said Janey. The room that was now the spare room was the only part of the flat with nothing broken or falling to bits in it.

Instead of dancing on the ashes of a down-at-heel, deserted old lady with a broken heart and housemaid's knee, Janey was inhabiting the former suite of a *femme fatale*.

'How come I thought that she was so sad then? I mean why did she . . . Are you completely sure?' she asked her mother.

'Quite sure,' her mother answered. 'Is it upsetting for you, somehow?'

'It's given me a bit of a shock, that's all.'

All the while the normal man had been making the tea. It was quarter to three. Janey put the rest of the custard creams on a plate and the cakes that had been baked on the Friday for the homeless which, though past their best, retained a certain charm. She put the geranium to one side and put the cornflowers in water. And the three of them ate this little meal together, chatting politely about Norman March.

'He sounds like a very extraordinary man from what you both say,' Edward told them.

'No, that's not quite the right word for him. He was an ordinary man, only a very good one,' Janey said.

'Who wants to be extraordinary when you can be ordinary, anyway,' said Mrs March. 'I, for one, have fought hard these past years to be normal.'

The three of them laughed together. 'Seeing as it's a special day I thought we might have a little whiskey in our tea,' Mrs March said and, taking a half bottle of Scotch from her bag, she poured half a capful into her own cup and some into Janey's cup and slightly more into the man's which was already half empty.

He poured out some more tea. 'In that case we ought

to have a toast,' he said.

'I know,' Janey nearly shouted, 'a toast to being normal.'

'Here's to being normal,' said Mrs March.

'Being normal,' said Edward Oxley, shrugging his shoulders.

'Ing normal,' said Janey.

Chink went the china. Janey raised her cup again.

'Normal,' she said. 'To being normal.'

'That's it,' Mrs March said.

'Certainly is,' Edward Oxley agreed. 'I can't stand neurotic people.'

No one spoke for a minute or so.

'Funny old world,' said the older woman.

'I know,' the younger woman answered.

'That's that then,' the man chipped in.

'Right.'

'Right.'

'Right.' The man laughed.

'Sorry, but I'm having the last word,' said Janey.

'OK.'

'Go on then,' said the man, taking her hand.

Janey took a deep breath, drew courage from the words on the storage jars, OATS, FLOUR, RICE, BEANS, RAISINS, TEA, COFFEE, took in the sight of her battered arm, her batty mother in the flowery dress, the custard creams and the geranium and the funny man stroking her fingers. The cathedral clock struck three. She swallowed and, closing her eyes, she summoned up a picture of her father's smiling face, 'Norm all,' she said.